Blaze™

The White Star Continuity

Book 1

ANGELS AND OUTLAWS

by

Lori Wilde

The legend begins… Thieves, lovers, scoundrels and saviors: good guys and bad surround Cass Richards and Sam Mason. Sam's a cop with a case involving stolen gems, but it's Cass—his assistant *and* prime suspect— who may be his prize catch….

HIDDEN GEMS by Carrie Alexander,
available February, Book 2

CAUGHT by Kristin Hardy,
available March, Book 3

INTO TEMPTATION by Jeanie London,
available April, Book 4

FULL CIRCLE by Shannon Hollis,
available May, Book 5

DESTINY'S HAND by Lori Wilde,
available June, Book 6

Blaze™

Dear Reader,

What if a legend-shrouded ancient amulet belonging to tragic star-crossed lovers and reputed to possess magical powers resurfaced in modern-day New York?

What if there are also dark forces, fueled by a dangerous obsession, seeking the amulet for personal greed and satisfaction?

And what if six women, all pure of heart and ready for true love, get caught up in the hunt for this special object, only to discover that it will dramatically alter their lives forever?

This intriguing scenario provides the framework for an action-packed six-book series that promises thrills, chills, twists and turns and of course, lots of steamy, red-hot romance.

The action kicks off in *Angels and Outlaws* when The White Star amulet is stolen from the exclusive Stanhope auction house in Manhattan and Detective Sergeant Sam Mason is assigned to the case. What Sam discovers about The White Star shocks him and puts gorgeous public relations representative Cass Richards at the top of his suspect list. Will true love win out?

Don't miss a single story in this series as it builds to an exciting and unexpected conclusion in *Destiny's Hand*.

Enjoy the ride!
Lori Wilde

ANGELS AND OUTLAWS

Lori Wilde

HARLEQUIN®

TORONTO • NEW YORK • LONDON
AMSTERDAM • PARIS • SYDNEY • HAMBURG
STOCKHOLM • ATHENS • TOKYO • MILAN • MADRID
PRAGUE • WARSAW • BUDAPEST • AUCKLAND

To Kathryn Lye—Thanks for all your incredibly hard work on this project. Only you understand how much this means.

ISBN 0-373-79234-4

ANGELS AND OUTLAWS

Copyright © 2006 by Laurie Vanzura.

www.eHarlequin.com

Printed in U.S.A.

The Legend Begins

Thousands of years ago in a faraway desert
kingdom lived two young princesses named Anan and
Batu. Anan was the older sister destined to inherit
the throne, but Batu was the prettier of the two
with her dark, almond eyes and her thick black hair.
While Anan was being groomed to take over her royal
duties, Batu was allowed to play freely. Her favorite
playmate was Egmath, the son of the bravest soldier
in the king's army.

Late one afternoon, as Batu and Egmath were
frolicking among the cypress trees on the outskirts
of the village, Egmath noticed the tiny buds on her
chest blooming beneath her robe and began teasing her
about them. Embarrassed by the odd changes in her
body and by Egmath's gentle jokes, Batu ran away
and hid herself among the sand dunes.

She felt confused. Why had his comments upset her
so? Until now, they'd joked and teased and poked fun
at each other about everything. What had changed?
Why did she feel so self-conscious? She ducked her
head, crossed her arms over her chest, willed the
strange bumps away and just kept running.

Alarmed that he'd hurt his best friend's feelings and worried that Batu had gone out into the desert alone with no water, Egmath went in search of her. He walked through the heated sand, calling her name, calling out a heartfelt apology, pleading with Batu to show herself. He crested one dune after another, moving farther and farther away from the village, but no Batu.

Evening crept over the horizon and young Egmath's fear and guilt grew deeper with each darkening second. The wind buffeted him and blew sand in his face, tossing his pleas into the twilight. She would never hear him now. Time passed. Stars speckled the sky.

"Batu, Batu, where are you?" he cried.

He thought he heard a jackal's low yipping, but he couldn't be sure. Panic pulled Egmath faster into the desert night. He stumbled, fell on his face, got up and kept trudging up a high dune. When he reached the summit and peered down into the basin below, terror gripped his heart.

There stood Batu, surrounded by a pack of snarling, hungry jackals.

Egmath had no idea what to do. He had no weapon, and the village was too far away. If he left to go find help, the jackals would surely attack before he could return. It was up to him and him alone to save her.

Batu hadn't seen him. She stared at the horrible creatures, frozen with fear, trapped, unable to move. The jackals edged closer in a slowly advancing circle.

Egmath swallowed hard, calling up every ounce of courage he possessed. His father had taught him there was nothing more important than honor and bravery. But how could one young boy hope to fight off eight slobbering jackals? This then was his first test as a man. He would save Batu or die trying.

Armed with nothing more than his love for Batu, Egmath let out a fierce, angry scream, waved his arms wildly above his head and charged down the dune.

The jackals, frightened by the brave young warrior, turned and ran away into the darkness.

Egmath reached Batu. His heart was pounding and he could barely breathe. He was so scared.

"You saved my life," Batu whispered.

He put his arms around her and held her close. "We must hurry to the village. Before the jackals come back."

Batu was trembling so hard she could not walk.

"I'll carry you," Egmath said.

He picked her up and she wrapped her legs around his waist and dropped her head onto his shoulder.

Their chests were pressed tightly together. She could feel the steady strum of his heart beneath hers. He was her savior, her hero.

When at last they reached the copse of cypress tress, Egmath set her down, took her hands in his and under the starlit sky, looked her straight in the eyes. "I'm so sorry for hurting your feelings," he murmured. "I should never have teased you."

"I should not have taken offense. I was silly. Thank you for caring enough to come after me."

They stared into each other's faces, and even though they were mere children they both knew they were fated to be together.

Egmath leaned in and tentatively, tenderly brushed his lips against Batu's for their very first kiss.

And in that same moment a falling star streaked across the sky, throwing itself like an angled spar— darting a brilliant white, yellow and blue. Sealing their kiss. Sealing their destiny.

Egmath and Batu, forever always.

TO BE CONTINUED…

Prologue

RIGHT OR WRONG, he must possess her.

Stealthily, Jean Luc Allard, professional jewel thief, crept from the shadows of the silent auction house, intent on one thing and one thing only.

The surveillance camera mounted overhead whispered as it rotated to scan the perimeter, but Jean knew how to avoid detection. Strategically placed, a high-powered magnet would disrupt the camera's feed.

For weeks, following the death of high-society heiress Zoey Zander, he'd researched every detail, learned every facet of the auction house's routine, preparing for the moment when his target would show up for bidding as part of the vast Zander estate. His instructions were clear. He must not allow her to go up for auction, no matter what the risk.

And now soon, very soon, Jean would hold her in his hands.

Excitement trembled his fingertips, anticipation sped his pulse. Nothing thrilled him like a daring heist. Nothing, that is, except what she represented.

The key to his future as a very wealthy man.

It was the most lucrative job he'd ever taken. He was so close, Jean could taste the money.

He'd heard the stories about her. She was legendary in his small world. According to rumor, only those who were pure of heart could possess her without falling under the curse.

Laughable.

His whole life had been cursed. There was nothing she could dish out that would top what he'd already suffered. Besides, he didn't believe in curses. Ruthlessness? Yes. Cruelty? *Oui.* Violence? A necessity in his trade. But fabled curses were no more real than children's fairy tales.

Silently, he crept toward the vault, barely able to restrain himself from rushing forward, when he heard a noise somewhere down the corridor.

He stepped back, pressed his body against the wall, stood stock still in the darkness and willed himself to disappear.

Don't move, don't make a single sound, don't even breathe.

Jean was dressed all in black from his black wool cap to his black leather sneakers. His hair was jet black and so were his eyes. Three days' worth of beard growth shadowed his jaw. He was one with the darkness, owned it. Holding his breath, he waited.

Footsteps drew nearer, but it was not the sound of the security guard's booted gait. The footfall was almost as furtive as his, sneaking quietly toward the vault without benefit of illumination.

Was someone else robbing the auction house?

Impossible.

Not on the same night he had chosen. Jean had discussed his heist with no one. A smart thief never talked about his jobs, no matter how tempting it might be to brag. Keeping his mouth shut was what had saved him from jail on many occasions and his ability to stay silent was the main reason his very wealthy, very well-connected employer had selected him for the job.

Could his enigmatic boss have hired someone else, just in case, to make sure Jean kept his end of the bargain? He ground his teeth, angered at his employer's lack of trust. Was there truly no honor among thieves?

Then again, maybe he was jumping to conclusions. The contents of Zoey Zander's estate had been extensively detailed in the newspaper. The woman had been wealthy enough to cause thieves on three continents to salivate, and the fact she had no immediate heirs made her fortune that much more enticing.

Jean watched as a broad-shouldered man loomed in the hallway. His mind shot back to an early childhood memory of his father stumbling through their house along a seedy stretch of the Seine. *Come here, you son of a whore. Don't hide from me.* But Jean knew if he stayed hidden long enough his father would pass out in a drunken stupor and in the morning forget why he'd wanted to beat him in the first place. He'd learned to hide in plain sight, blending into the shadows, anchoring his fear down tight inside him.

When the stranger reached the door of the vault, he stopped and switched on a penlight.

Jean studied the man's face in the gloom, but did not recognize him. He was younger than Jean and dressed casually, but elegantly. Like the son of a rich man. The interloper punched a number into the coded key pad and the vault door clicked open.

Interesting.

Where had he gotten the code? Did he work for the auction house? Jean had planned on sabotaging the mechanisms of the vault door and then disengaging the internal alarm with a special device designed by his employer. An anti-anti-theft apparatus. But this poser had simply obtained access to the deactivation code.

Specifically what had he come after?

The man disappeared inside the vault, but left the door ajar.

Jean hung back for a second and then edged forward. Cautiously, he peered through the opening. The man quickly skirted the antiques, memorabilia and other large items of the Zoey Zander collection and headed straight for a tall, upright safe at the back of the room.

Suddenly what had seemed like an imposing obstacle—the unexpected appearance of this stranger—became a blessing in disguise. Jean would let this man do the hard work.

His excitement was back. It tasted sweet and edgy

against his tongue. His nose tingled with the smell of secrets, the tang of adrenaline.

The man stuck his penlight between his teeth and shone the thin beam on the lock. He spun the combination. The safe door popped open. Shoulders hunched, he dug inside, retrieved a fistful of jewels and stuffed them into a royal blue felt pouch he'd pulled from his jacket pocket.

Jean flexed his fingers, aching to touch her.

The man straightened, turned and for the first time saw Jean. He startled and then opened his mouth.

But he never got a word out.

Jean slammed the butt of his Luger hard against the side of the other man's temple.

His eyes glassed over, his knees buckled and he went down.

Reaching out, Jean plucked the felt pouch from his hand as he fell. The penlight hit the floor beside him. Jean bent and picked it up, directed the light into the pouch. He ignored the rubies and emeralds and diamonds. His eyes were hungry for one thing and one thing only.

She smiled up at him, resplendent in the sliver of wan light. Smiled and winked and sparkled. She was perfect. Ivory in the shape of a five-pointed star with a hollow center.

He separated her from the other gems, but in the process, the pin of an onyx brooch pierced his thumb. He cursed softly, brought his thumb to his mouth and tasted blood.

He dropped the brooch and the rest of the jewels on

top of the downed man. The interloper might as well have something for his troubles besides a throbbing headache when he awoke.

Jean's eyes turned back to the amulet, now cradled in his palm, compelled by her allure. His breathing stopped. How could such a beauty be cursed?

Romantic rubbish.

Never mind the foolish legend. At long last she was his. And she was going to make him rich beyond his wildest imagination.

How he loved her.

His White Star amulet.

1

DON'T LOOK DOWN.

Cassandra "Cass" Richards, assistant public relations representative to the haute couture house of Isaac Vincent, stood trembling on a window ledge eight floors above Broadway in Manhattan's garment district. One wrong move and she would plummet like a runway model's weight two weeks before the spring collection debut.

Suddenly, shimmying after her Hermès scarf, which had caught on one of the brownstone's grim-faced gargoyles, seemed more and more like a very bad idea. The brisk spring breeze had whisked it off her neck when she'd leaned out the open window to wave goodbye to her best friend, Marissa Suarez, who was heading off to the Caribbean with her boyfriend and had stopped by the office to leave Cass a key to her apartment just in case.

Wind whipped up her smart pink pencil skirt, sending a bone chill up her spine and causing her to realize that wearing a g-string thong today was probably not the brightest impulse she'd ever had.

And let's face it, in her much-prized four-inch Manolo Blahnik pink patent leather Mary Janes that had set her back a full month's salary, she was at a distinct disadvantage for navigating the eight-inch-wide cement outcropping.

How did she keep getting herself into these ridiculous fixes? She bit down on her bottom lip and eyed the traffic below.

Her head reeled dizzily.

Don't look down.

She was pressed flush against the side of the building, arms splayed out at her sides, the coveted Hermès scarf clutched tightly in her right hand. She wrinkled her nose at the thought of what the dirty bricks were doing to her glamorous outfit.

When she'd first climbed onto the ledge it hadn't seemed so scary because her attention had been fixed on the scarf. She had leaned out, never meaning to actually end up on the protrusion, but then she'd discovered her reach wasn't quite long enough. She'd winnowed her hips through the window frame just to give her an extra couple of inches.

Close, but not close enough.

Don't look down.

She'd held tightly to the frame, swung her legs around and then edged out onto the ledge. Two, three steps maximum was all it had taken to reach that first gargoyle.

Unfortunately, just as Cass had grasped for the recalcitrant scarf, the wind grabbed it again and fluttered it over to a second gargoyle a good four feet farther on down the ledge.

She hadn't thought about anything except how many lunches she'd had to skip to afford the damned thing. Now, one wrong move and she wouldn't have to worry about missed lunches or expensive scarves or passersby staring up her skirt ever again.

Please get me out of this alive and I promise, promise, promise I'll be less impetuous in future, she bargained with the heavens.

She got her answer in the form of raindrops spattering on her head.

Terrific.

Apparently, there would be no divine intervention forthcoming today. Her salvation was up to her. Thank God her mascara was waterproof, but her hair was doomed to frizz.

"You can do this," she told herself. "You got out here, you can get back. One step at a time."

She made a tentative move toward the window she'd come out of, knees trembling with cold and fear. The heel of one stiletto hung on a crack in the cement ledge. Cass stumbled and for one horrifying moment she thought she was done for, but an updraft of wind pushed her into the brownstone instead of away from it.

Don't look down.

Her heart pounded and her stomach roiled. She was never going to get off this precipice and all for a damned scarf.

Ah, but it wasn't just any scarf.

She'd purchased the Hermès two days after her older sister, Morgan, had closed on a magnificent six-bedroom dream home in Connecticut that she planned on filling with children.

Cass had been happy for Morgan, who was married to the most perfect guy—the sort of down-to-earth, good-hearted man that Cass figured she'd never find for herself. Not that she was looking. Adam was a Wall Street investment banker with a flair for making money and a penchant for spending it on his wife, but Cass wasn't jealous of her sister's husband or their grand home or their affluent suburban lifestyle.

No, she'd maxed out her Visa on the scarf because wearing expensive, gorgeous things made her feel better about herself. With her parents bragging about Morgan and pointedly asking when Cass was going to settle down and get married and start producing grandchildren, she'd felt pressured and overshadowed.

And the Hermès had done its job, snapping her right out of her funk.

Truthfully, she liked her life exactly as it was. She wasn't on the prowl for Mr. Right. She was having too much fun being young and single and dating in the most vibrant city in the world. She'd snagged her dream job at Isaac Vincent. She adored her fourth-floor walkup in Tribeca. Loved that she never had to cook. Treasured her freedom to come and go as she pleased and spend her money on whatever she wanted.

Including exorbitantly priced fashion accessories.

She wasn't even sure that she ever wanted the husband,

the kids and the house. Deep down inside, she doubted she could handle such an awesome responsibility as a family of her own. Best leave that to dutiful Morgan.

But still, sometimes…*sometimes*…she couldn't help wondering what she was missing out on.

And when Cass got those itchy feelings, Cass went shopping.

Hence the Hermès.

Made from the purest silk twill. Paisley patterned and pleated and colored with the truest dyes. The hues in the scarf collaborated with a dozen different outfits and she wore it often. It wasn't as if she'd bought the scarf and then shoved it in the back of her closet. That scarf made her feel rich and important and worthy.

Yet here she was, on the verge of trading her life for a scrap of fancy material.

What was wrong with this picture?

She hazarded another look down, saw that a knot of gawkers had gathered and were pointing up.

Oh, joy.

She groaned as fresh nausea rolled through her. And then she saw the television crew.

The wind gusted again, whistling around the side of the brownstone. *Could* people see up her skirt? Cass blushed.

Okay, it was official. Things couldn't get any suckier. She was stuck out on a window ledge, in the rain, inches from death and after the noon news hit the air everyone in New York was going to know what kind of panties she wore.

DETECTIVE SERGEANT SAM MASON followed the collective gaze of the murmuring crowd, spied the woman clinging to the ledge of the building he'd been about to enter and his blood ran cold.

He counted the floors. Eight stories up. Bizarre. He'd been headed for the eighth floor.

"Jump," hollered a punk kid in the crowd.

"Jump, jump." Another snickering teen picked up the chant as if the possibility of someone's death was just a big joke.

"Shut up," Sam commanded, scowling then flashing his badge at the clueless teens. Had people lost *all* sense of common decency? "Or I'll arrest you on the spot."

The punks sobered and did as he said. Sam swung his gaze back to the jumper.

She'd picked a miserable day for it. The light sprinkles that had greeted him three blocks ago when he'd gotten off the subway had changed into a steady drizzle. The wind whipped wild and biting.

Honey, he thought, and mentally willed her back inside, *whoever the guy is who's driven you to this, he's just not worth it.*

She took a step sideways toward the open window several feet to her left. He prayed she was reconsidering her suicide bid. Then she stumbled and almost lost her balance.

The crowd gasped.

By some hand of fate, she managed at the last moment to correct herself. Sam's heart stilled and a flash of déjà vu fisted his gut. In his mind's eye ten years dropped away and it was his second week on the job as an NYPD rookie beat cop.

That woman had been a jumper, too, distraught over the breakup of her marriage, perched precariously on the Brooklyn Bridge. Sam had sweet-talked, he'd cajoled, he'd made promises he couldn't really keep and he had sweated it.

The woman seemed to calm down. To grow peaceful and quiet. Sam believed he'd won. He'd held her in his hands for a brief moment, arrogantly thinking that he had saved her. Then she'd met his gaze with her sad, soulful blue eyes that were too big for her face and she'd simply let go, taking that one fatal step backward into the black abyss.

He'd had nightmares about her for weeks afterward, waking in the middle of the night sweaty and guilty. Cringing, Sam briefly closed his eyes, blocking out the memory.

No. He could not, would not, let it happen again. This time he was older, wiser, more experienced, less full of himself. He was being given a second chance. This time he would save her.

He bound into the building, his brain speeding ahead of him, mapping out rescue strategies. One of the elevators was at the ground floor.

"Hold the door," he shouted, but the doors bumped closed just as he reached the lift.

"Dammit," he cursed, frantically jabbing the up button repeatedly. He swung his gaze to the lighted numbers above the remaining elevators. None of them were near the ground floor.

Swearing again, he tore around the corner in search of the stairwell.

"Sir, sir, excuse me, sir."

The lobby receptionist he'd ignored came chasing after him, her heels striking snap-snap-snap against the cement floor. She caught him at the stairwell door.

"Sir, you must check in at the security desk before you can go up."

"NYPD," he growled at the woman. "You've got a jumper on the eighth floor."

Startled, she raised a hand to her throat. "Oh my goodness."

"Call the fire department and tell them what's happening," Sam ordered.

She stood there stunned.

"Now!" he shouted and shouldered through the door into the stairwell.

He took the steps two at a time, the vein in his forehead throbbing from exertion. Less than a minute later he burst onto the eighth floor, chest heaving, sweat on his brow. People in the hallway turned to stare, but he ignored them.

Gotta save her. Can't let it happen again.

He had a chance for redemption. He wouldn't let her slip through his fingers, wouldn't be responsible for sending someone else over the edge.

Sam rushed past several offices that he knew weren't in the right spot. He zipped through a great room thronged with ribbon-thin models in various stages of undress. Any other time and he might have been tempted to ogle, but not today.

Designers and tailors and seamstresses bustled to and fro. Bolts of lush colorful fabric littered tables, with bows and lace and sewing supplies scattered about. Sam's eyes darted around the room. Clearly, no one realized that a young woman, quite possibly one of their coworkers, was perched on the window ledge preparing to take her own life.

This was taking too long. He had to get to her before she jumped.

He flung open the door of the next office he came to, angling straight for the window. The sign on the door identified it as Isaac Vincent's public relations office. The person Sam had come here to interview about a string of high-end home robberies worked in this very office.

Weird coincidence.

Except Sam didn't believe in coincidences. But he had no time to piece the puzzle together.

The office lay empty.

Sirens shrieked. Thank God the fire department was on the way.

Pulse racing, he rushed to the window and poked his head out, just as his old childhood fear blindsided him like a blow to the brain.

Sam Mason was terrified of heights.

2

"HI, I'M SAM. What's your name?"

Excuse me?

Very carefully Cass turned her head to meet the astute dark gray eyes of the obviously insane man sticking his head out of her office window and chatting her up as if they were at a singles meet-and-greet.

"Um, Cass Richards," she replied because she'd been raised to be polite. What she really wanted was to tell him to take a hike. Staying on the window ledge was chore enough—she didn't need him distracting her.

"Cass Richards?" There was a strange tone in his voice.

"Yeah."

"Cass, listen to me, whatever is driving you out on the window ledge is fixable. Suicide is not the solution."

Suicide?

What on earth was he babbling about? He thought she wanted to kill herself? Well, that was just dumb. What she wanted was to get back inside, find a blow dryer and a hot latte.

Cass started to reach up a hand to push her damp hair

off her face, but the movement made her teeter precariously on her high heels. She glanced down again, saw firemen running around blowing up one of those big inflatable jumpy thingies stuntmen used in the movies and positioning it directly below her.

The building seemed to sway.

Horns honked. The crowd was shouting up at her, but she couldn't hear what they were saying above the rumble of the fire engines and the wind whistling around the corner of the brownstone.

"Look at me, Cass," Sam said, his voice low and soothing.

She snapped her gaze to his rugged face, grateful to have something, anything to look at besides the traffic below.

He pinned her to the ledge with his eyes. They were solid and deep. How could she fall as long as he was looking at her like that?

You won't fall, his expression declared. *I won't let you.*

And for some unfathomable reason, she believed the promise on his face.

"Let's talk about it," he gently cajoled.

"Okay." Why not? Anything to get her mind off the fact that she was inches away from cracking her skull into multiple pieces.

"Is this about a man?" he asked.

Wasn't that just like a guy to assume she'd want to fling herself to the pavement over some man? She was half tempted to tell him it was about a woman simply to see surprise spark his eyes.

"FYI," she said. "I have absolutely no intention of jumping."

"Good," he said. "That's very good. So this is just a plea for help. To get someone to listen. To have your pain heard."

"Nooo."

Who was this guy? And where in the heck had he come from? She hadn't ordered a touchy-feely buttinsky psychologist to go. What she wanted was some big, strong strapping hero to throw her over his shoulder and walk her safely off this damned ledge.

She eyed him.

Under the circumstances she shouldn't have noticed his short sandy brown hair, obviously styled by a discount barber, but the fashionista in her wouldn't be stilled. A great haircut would go a long way in accenting his interesting cheekbones and some blond highlights would coax a bit of color into his desert gray eyes.

He leaned out the window. His shoulders were broad and his chest strapping. No matter what idealistic sentiment he might have just expressed in order to keep her from jumping off the ledge, clearly he was not by nature the sort of man who got in touch with his inner feelings or indulged in hundred dollar haircuts.

The set of his shoulders, the nonchalant way he was dressed in rumpled khakis and an untucked buttondown blue chambray shirt told her he was a working class Joe. Salt of the earth, this one.

"What *is* it about, Cass?"

She raised the hand she'd fisted around the scarf.

"Ah," he said. "I get it. You're up here for a cause. Taking a stand against some political or economical or social injustice."

"Nooo."

Boy was he off base. She would have shaken her head but she was afraid the movement would make her even dizzier then she already was.

"I'm listening, Cass. You can tell me what's bothering you."

"Well, gee thanks for the concern, Sam, but nothing's bothering me."

"Then why are you on that ledge?"

He looked so sincere, so worried for her safety that she felt a little silly saying it. "I came out for the Hermès."

"Pardon?" He appeared confused and she realized the problem.

"I'm talking about the scarf."

"What about the scarf?"

"It blew off my neck."

As Cass watched, his face changed from earnest to perplexed. "Let me get this straight. You climbed out on a window ledge for a scarf?"

"Eight stories really doesn't seem that high until you're out here."

He was looking at her as if she was the most foolish woman on the planet and actually right now, that's exactly how she felt.

"It's a Hermès," she explained.

"For a scarf?" he repeated.

"A very expensive scarf."

"Lady," he growled, all trace of the understanding, considerate, suicide-jumper-talker-downer vanishing, "you're nuts."

"Gee, that's not very nice."

"What kind of shallow, narcissistic, materialistic, egocentric…"

"You can give it a rest. I get the picture. If I'm a jumper then you're all sympathetic and helpful but if I'm just…"

"Blond," he supplied.

She glared. "I was going to say *rash*."

"This is way past rash and well on the road to foolhardy."

Cass sniffed. He was right, but she didn't have to admit it. "Apparently we don't share the same value system."

"Hell," he said. "I don't think we even share the same solar system."

"Be that as it may," she said snippily, "I did come out here and now I'm too nervous to climb back in, so if you'd be so kind as to please go find a nice fireman or policeman to come rescue me, I'd appreciate it."

"I am a policeman."

"You don't look like a policeman."

"I'm a detective. I don't wear a uniform."

She groaned inwardly and rolled her eyes. Just her luck. She'd drawn a cop who was a bad dresser with an attitude to match.

He held out his hand. "Come back in."

"I can't."

"Why not?"

"Every time I try to move I get dizzy and start to lose my balance."

He eyed the ground and then cussed under his breath.

What? Panic shot through her. Did he know something she didn't?

"What is it? What's wrong?"

"Nothing's wrong."

"Then why are you cursing?"

"If it weren't for you I'd be having Starbucks and Krispy Kremes right about now."

"Shoo," she said, but didn't dare motion with her hands. She'd already moved around too much. "Go on. Go shoot your cholesterol through the roof. Sorry to ruin your day."

"Hang on. I'll come get you."

"I don't want your help."

"Tough. You've got it." With that, he grimly thrust himself out the window and onto the ledge.

She felt his movements vibrate straight up through the concrete precipice and she tensed. He had a pragmatic way about him, the aura of a man doing his duty whether he liked it or not.

She didn't like being his duty.

He came toward her as casually as if he were walking his dog in Central Park instead of traversing a ledge no wider than a shoebox. She stood in awe. Where had he acquired such utter self-confidence? He looked as if he owned the world and everything in it.

Including her.

Hell, it had even stopped raining.

He wasn't at all like the well-bred, well-dressed men she normally hung out with. Cass's breath escaped her lungs in a sharp, inexplicable gasp. A shiver slipped down her spine and she had no idea if it was due to the danger she was in or to the man heading for her.

His face was rugged, chiseled. His mouth determined. His eyes incisive. He was the sort of man who made a woman feel safe.

Since when have you ever opted for safe?

Uncontrollably, her gaze fell to the street. Since now. Her knees weakened.

"Look at me, Cass," Sam, the sexy detective, commanded.

The fire trucks were a swirl of red, the crowd a muddle of melted faces. Her fingers cramped from holding on to the wall and she felt as if she was coming unraveled at the seams.

"Look at me."

Slowly, she raised her chin and met his eyes.

"Atta girl. Hold on. I'm almost there."

She'd never been attracted to rough-hewn, macho types before. Give her suave and debonair any day. Except right now, she was mighty glad to have him.

To distract herself she imagined him in a tuxedo at one of Isaac Vincent's exclusive parties, drinking champagne and making idle chitchat with supermodels and fashion designers.

Cass was creative, but no matter how hard she tried

that was one image that refused to be conjured. This guy belonged at a bar called O'Malley's or Mac-Dougall's with a mug of warm beer in front of him and a knot of buddies chalking pool cues and making off-color jokes about the waitresses.

But she could see him as a proud Scottish pirate at the bow of his sailing ship gazing out at the new land he was about to pillage. Suddenly, in her mind's eye, she was a maiden in that faraway land being captured by her conqueror and made to service him in so many shameful, pleasurable ways.

A vision of their entwined bodies muscled out her fear. She pictured Sam's heavy, potent hands caressing her heated skin with tender urgency…his clever gun-metal gray eyes assembling secret knowledge about her body. He noted what his touch did to her, what made her arch her back, what caused her to moan. In an intense and surreal flash of awareness Cass saw his hard-muscled body covering hers, guiding her to a fevered pitch time and time again.

A warm tingle gripped her and her mouth filled with moisture.

Was she perverted? Or was this a perfectly natural response to hovering on the verge of death? Perhaps it was preferable that one's last thoughts should be centered on a marvelous sexual fantasy rather than the gruesome alternative.

By the time Sam reached her they were both breathing hard and when his eyes met hers, she could have sworn it was the devil himself peering deep into her.

The air around her solidified with a thick, masculine heat and Cass fought off the urge to squirm.

"Take my hand."

She hesitated. Not because she didn't want to be rescued, but for a split second there, she didn't know which was more treacherous. Touching him or staying out here on the ledge.

His grip was hot and reassuring. She looked him in the eyes. His smile was tight, the outline of his lips white. He'd made the trip down the rain slick ledge look easy, but it was not.

Her legs, strained by the high heels, the cold wet wind and a big dose of fear, quivered precariously.

"One step at a time."

"I can't."

"Yes, you can."

A fireman on the street hollered something up at them through a bullhorn, but Cass couldn't hear anything except the voice inside her head telling her that it was all over, that she was going to die and she better make the best of the short time she had left.

What would Sam do if she asked him to kiss her?

"Ignore the guy with the bullhorn," Sam said. "Listen to me. I'll get you out of this."

She looked down and immediately swooned. Her knees crumpled and if Sam hadn't had his fingers locked tightly around her wrist she would have been lost.

"Close your eyes."

"What!"

"Close your eyes and listen to me."

But she couldn't. She was too panicked, too scared to trust a man she didn't know. She kept looking down and down and down.

Her vision swirled. She cried out and grabbed for Sam's shirt.

"Cass, no," he shouted. "You'll knock me off balance."

But his warning came too late.

Together they tumbled off the ledge.

HER BUTT WAS IN HIS PALM.

Something very akin to excitement stirred his blood, accelerated his breathing, hummed his heartbeat.

They'd fallen eight stories locked in each other's arms and the only thing Sam could think about was Cass Richards's butt.

That cute butt saved him from his fear of heights, from his fear of falling, from darn near the fear of everything.

Her skirt was hiked up and his palm was splayed across her bare bottom. Lord love her, she was wearing a thong.

And it was the softest, sweetest bottom he'd ever held. She was a slender woman, not supermodel slim, but not fleshy either.

Except for that glorious fanny. It was full and kneadable and splendid.

And his body responded in a solely masculine way. Talk about unprofessional.

They landed, with a tight controlled bounce, on the giant airbag the fire department had inflated underneath the eighth floor office. They were positioned squarely in the middle—a textbook landing—and still a good ten feet off the ground and Sam's hand was on Cass's delectable backside.

It was a sensation he knew he'd remember for the rest of his life.

"Get your hand off my ass," she snapped, and rolled away from him.

So much for pleasant dreams.

"Sorry," he said, but he wasn't the least bit contrite.

He deserved some small compensation for battling his dread fear of heights in order to rescue her. She had no idea how much that little trip had cost him. How hard he'd had to fake his bravery in order to force himself out onto that ledge.

Or how much landing alive in the airbag with her meant to him. He'd faced his fear and in doing so he'd saved her life.

Well, okay, technically the fire department had saved her, but if he hadn't told the receptionist to call the fire department they both would have been wearing halos and playing harps by now.

Or the way your mind is working, wearing horns and dancing with pitchforks.

Right.

A fireman was already at the edge of the airbag, reaching out, helping her slide off. By the time Sam worked his way to the edge, Cass was standing on the street, surrounded by reporters, looking like a princess holding court.

Sam rolled his eyes.

He should have known. Once upon a time he'd been married to a prima donna princess for nine, very long, miserable months. He knew far too well how the species operated.

No one gave him a second look and he found himself pushed back with the rest of the crowd, inconsequential as froth on a mug of beer. She was the consummate PR professional, making opportunity out of a mishap—milking the media coverage for all she was worth, smiling to the bystanders, flirting with the cameramen, poised as a movie star.

She craved attention. That much was clear. Question was, how far would she go to get it?

It was only after she'd been whisked away in an awaiting limousine—he had no idea where that had come from, but prima donna princesses did have their minions—Sam realized he'd never gotten to tell her why he'd come to see her in the first place.

Someone had been stealing valuable jewelry from Cass Richards's circle of affluent friends and Sam had to question if Cass really had been on the ledge after a scarf. It was a thin story. Could a guilty conscience actually have been the driving force behind her impromptu perch instead?

3

"CASS, DID YOU HEAR what I just said?"

"Huh?" Cass raised her chin, looking up from the antique Christmas plates she'd been sorting in the basement of her older sister's quaint and cozy antique shop in Fairfield, Connecticut. She wiped the dust off Ten Lords a Leaping with a damp cloth—wondering quite incidentally what all the leaping was about—and blinked at Morgan.

"Is something the matter? You've been distracted all morning."

"Just thinking about that fall I took off the eighth-floor window ledge."

And about Sam's big masculine hand on my fanny.

Damn, the sexual drought she'd been in was wreaking havoc with her imagination. Truth was she hadn't been able to stop thinking about him. That low, steady, horse-whisperer kind of voice he possessed made you feel as if you could trust every single word he said.

Morgan shuddered. "I'd think you'd want to forget all about that. Isn't that why you volunteered to help me out this weekend? To get away from the city and being reminded of what happened."

"Yes, yes, you're right. So what was it that you just asked?"

"Are you still seeing Marcos? I'm having a dinner party Friday week and…"

"Dumped him," Cass said quickly.

"Really? Already? You'd only been going with him what, a month?"

"Believe me, a month was enough."

"But he seemed so nice and his family is in the social registry and he's so good looking and so…"

"Clingy."

"You think any man who wants to be exclusive is clingy." Morgan took a box cutter, slit the tape on a large cardboard box, pushed back the flaps and began carefully taking out rare antique books.

"He was talking the *m* word after less than a month of dating and we'd never even slept together. Now that's moving way too fast for me."

"He asked you to marry him?" Morgan looked up in surprise.

"No, not *that m* word. He asked me to move in with him."

"I see why you had to dump him. Can't have a guy who'd actually want to be with you."

"Ha, ha. And this is going to make you feel bad for making fun of me, but after the news coverage of my unfortunate window ledge episode, Bunnie Bernaldo told me Marcos has been spreading rumors up and down Long Island that *he* dumped *me* and I was so distraught I would have thrown myself off the Isaac Vincent building over the breakup if Sam hadn't intervened. Of course anyone who knows me knows what a crock of bull that is. But can you believe that? I would never throw myself off a building over a man. The loss of a great pair of shoes, now maybe."

"Sam?" Morgan arched an eyebrow.

"The cop that helped me down from the ledge the hard way."

"You're on a first-name basis?"

Cass shrugged. "Well, that's how he introduced himself. As Sam."

"You like him," Morgan teased.

"Come on. I saw him once and that was under duress."

"Still." Morgan nodded. "You like him."

"Not that much. He was kind of a smart aleck when he heard about the Hermès."

"Is he cute?"

"Children don't scream in horror when he walks past if that's what you mean."

"Cass's got a new boyfriend."

"Shut up, I do not."

She wanted out of this conversation. The sooner the better. Cass spied a very old, ornately carved wooden box perched on a highboy in the corner. She got up, dusted off her hands and crossed the room to pick it up.

"What's this?"

Morgan swiveled her head in Cass's direction. "Intriguing, isn't it. I found it hidden in a secret drawer of an antique dresser I bought along with the shop."

The box was intricately hand-carved with various patterns. Cass traced a finger over the carvings. They may have been symbols, she wasn't sure, though they looked as if they were some kind of ancient hieroglyphics.

Was it a code? The idea excited her.

From the box emanated the faint scent of some rich, exotic spice. She held the box to her ear and shook it but neither heard nor felt anything inside.

"What's in it?"

"I don't know."

"Let's open it." Cass loved secrets and surprises and encrypted code games and this was just the thing that she needed to take her mind off sexy Detective Sam.

"We can't."

"Oh, Morgan, don't be such a party-pooper. It belongs to you. Why can't we open it?"

"There's no key."

"Let's jimmy the lock." She turned the box over and realized there was no keyhole at all.

Strange. A box with no opening.

"Don't you think I've tried? In fact I've developed a fascination with it. Who it belonged to, what happened to them, what's inside. Adam says I'm obsessed."

"Are you?"

Morgan shrugged, didn't admit to anything. But Cass saw how her eyes gleamed when she looked at the box. "We could jam a screwdriver into it, pop it open like a clam."

"The box is really old. Hundreds of years, maybe even more. I don't dare risk doing anything that could destroy it."

"Bummer." Cass sighed, put the box back on the highboy and returned to sit cross-legged in front of the knickknacks she'd been cataloging.

They worked in companionable silence for a few minutes and then Morgan said, "You do realize that your longest relationship was with a guy who lived in London and you only saw him a few times a year."

Cass smiled. "Oh yes, Nigel. He was the best of the lot."

"Because he didn't get in your hair. That's the way you like them, tall, dark and absent. Admit it, Cass. You're commitmentphobic."

"Why do you consider me commitmentphobic simply because I'm not lining up to get married and have babies?" Cass asked. "I'm not commitmentphobic. I just haven't found the right guy."

"What was wrong with Gregory Henderson? He was really nice and smart enough to keep up with you."

Cass waved a hand. "He had a high-pitched voice. Come on, could you face 'til-death-do-you-part' with a guy who sounds like he's constantly inhaling helium?"

Morgan tried not to smile. "What about Ross Roosevelt?"

"The man wore a size twenty-two shoe. And before you ask, no, the myth about men with big feet having other big parts is not true—in fact it seemed to be quite the opposite in his case."

"Pete Kerns?"

"Pul-leaze, he talked with his mouth full."

"You're minimizing their good points and maximizing their bad."

"What? I should marry the first halfway decent guy who crosses my path simply because he is halfway decent?" Cass shook her head. "Nope. Sorry. If I get married it will have to be to someone who blows my socks off with Fourth-of-July fireworks both in bed and out."

"You're romanticizing marriage. It's not like that. You have to work at it."

"That's why I don't want to commit. I don't want to have to work at being happy. I'm plenty happy all on my own. Besides, you have to remember, not everyone is as lucky as you, Morgan," Cass retorted. Her sister had been married for a decade. She had no idea what it was like trying to find a good man these days. "Not everyone snags the perfect guy right from the get-go."

Morgan pursed her lips and dropped her gaze. "Adam's not perfect."

"Of course he is."

Cass adored Adam. He was the big brother she'd never had. He was bright and polite and caring, made a great living and he was very good-looking. Her sister was so lucky.

"Nobody's perfect." Morgan's tone of voice surprised her.

"Are you guys having marital problems?" Cass asked.

The idea shocked her. Sure, Adam and Morgan had been married for ten years, but they'd always been rock solid. As far as Cass knew they'd never even really had a serious argument.

"No, no. Nothing like that, it's just…" Morgan let her words trail off.

"Just what?" Cass drew her knees to her chest and leaned forward.

"Adam's so busy with work and I've been preoccupied with opening the shop and given his long commute we don't have as much time together as I hoped when we bought this place." Morgan sighed. "I'm beginning to wonder if we're ever going to find time to start a family."

Cass felt melancholy. See there. That was one of the main reasons she didn't want a long-term relationship. The passion always fizzled. No matter how much two people loved each other. It was inevitable. But she wasn't one to dwell on problems for long. She was an action-oriented girl. If something was broke, well then you fixed it.

"Why are you here with me? You should be spending your Sunday with Adam."

Morgan sighed. "He's golfing with an important client."

"So why don't you take up golf?"

Her sister shot her a withering glance. "Yoga is as physical as I get."

"Maybe that's the problem." Cass grinned wickedly and started humming that old Olivia Newton-John song, "Physical."

"Easy for you to say. You're loaded with excess energy."

"Sorry," Cass apologized. "I didn't mean to make light of it."

"No, it's okay. I need to lighten up. In fact, I'm really glad you're here. You have a knack for making me see rainbows beyond the storm clouds."

Cass smiled at the compliment. "Have you tried fantasy role-playing? Bedroom toys? Sexy videos? I don't mean to brag but I could steer you in the right direction if you're interested."

"I'm not sure I'm ready for sex toys and naughty movies. I thought maybe a vacation."

"That's a great place to start. Got any locales in mind?"

Morgan ducked her head and Cass was surprised to realize her older sister was feeling shy. She probably felt awkward discussing her sex life.

"Actually," Morgan confessed. "I've been listening to French language tapes. I thought if I could speak a little French it might spice things up."

"Oooh la la."

"And then I saw this travel brochure advertising a week at a chateau in the Loire valley. The chateau used to be a military fortress. It has a drawbridge and a moat and everything. It's situated along the banks of a river. There's lush gardens and rolling woodlands. Cass, you should see the pictures. It's breathtaking and so romantic."

"Sounds to die for."

"I just hope it works," Morgan fretted.

"Things have gotten that stale?"

Morgan nodded and looked away, but not before Cass saw the darkening of concern in her eyes.

She gulped. Her big sister was always the one to comfort her. Now that the shoe was on the other foot she really didn't know how to reassure Morgan that everything was going to work out okay. Rather than deal with the awkward silence, Cass started rooting around in the stack of books Morgan had taken from the box, looking for something, anything to make her sister laugh.

"Hey, what's this?" Cass picked up a dusty old tome. It was just the sort of book Morgan would love, ancient and lore-riddled. "Look, it's in French."

Her ploy worked. Morgan glanced up, curiosity replacing the worry.

"Think you can translate it?" Cass passed the book to her.

Morgan took the thick volume, traced a finger over the aged lettering. "I've just started my lessons."

"Yeah, but you're a fast learner, Miss Top Ten Percent of her NYU graduate school class."

Morgan smiled. "All right. I'll give it a go."

Cass changed positions, scooting around until she was sitting knee to knee with her sister. They used to sit this way when they were kids, telling each other romantic fairy tales about stalwart knights and fair maidens and true, undying love. It felt good to sit with Morgan like this again. To remember what their relationship had been like before life had gotten in the way.

As a kid, Cass had always looked up to Morgan and tried to emulate her. But later, as her parents inevitably ended up comparing her to her older sister and she continually came up short, Cass found herself rebelling. She could never be Morgan, so why try?

Maybe that was one of the reasons she wasn't so keen on long-term relationships.

Morgan opened the cover and carefully thumbed through the pages. "It appears to be a text about ancient myths and legends."

"Ooh, what kind of legends?" Cass rubbed her palms together. This was getting intriguing.

Morgan frowned and studied the words. "I think it's got something to do with star-crossed lovers, but I can't say for sure. I've only started basic French."

"Excellent."

Morgan flipped more pages, and then stopped. "Hey, this looks familiar."

"What does?"

Morgan turned the book around so Cass could see the illustration of an elaborately detailed five-pointed star with a hollowed-out center. "Where have I seen this drawing before?"

Cass recognized it immediately, because the article had appeared in the fashion section of that morning's edition of the Sunday *New York Times,* right next to an ad for a deadly cute pair of boots on sale at Bergdorf Goodman's. She hadn't read the article but she had noticed the sale was going on through the following weekend.

"Hang on. I'll be right back."

She dashed upstairs to the antique shop where they'd had bagels and cream cheese for breakfast while reading the newspaper. She snatched up the arts and entertainment sections and hurried back down to the basement.

After spreading the newspaper out on the floor, Cass took the book from Morgan and laid it open next to the drawing in the paper.

They were identical.

The caption underneath the photograph read *Archaeological artifact, the White Star amulet, was listed among items stolen from the Zoey Zander estate after a midnight break-in at Stanhope's auction house.*

As Cass looked at the picture of the amulet, something warm tugged at her solar plexus. Inexplicably, she started thinking about Detective Sam again.

"It's the same amulet," Morgan said, running a finger along the lines in the book. "I do recognize the words 'white star' in this French text."

"*Très* cool." Cass grinned impishly. "We're involved in a jewel heist."

"We're not involved."

"We've found a mysterious old book just at the very same time the amulet is stolen."

"Slow down, Harriet the Spy, you're making grand leaps of logic."

"Still, you never know. The book might be helpful to the investigation. Maybe someone should take it to the police."

"Someone meaning you?"

"Sure. I could pop in the police station on my way to work tomorrow morning, leave the book with them. Do my civic duty."

"See that sexy detective who went out on the ledge for you."

"There is that." Cass grinned and snapped the book closed.

"ANY NEW LEADS on the Stanhope auction house robbery?" In the main corridor of the 39th Precinct, Sam caught up with his colleague, Carl Weston, one of the outgoing night shift detectives. Sam was on his way into the briefing room for Monday morning roll call, a cup of strong, black coffee clutched in his hand.

"You look like hell, bloodhound." Weston winked. Sam had earned the nickname for his acute sense of smell that had actually helped him solve a case once. "Must have been some wild weekend. Got any details for us married guys who live vicariously through you bachelors?"

Sam had spent the weekend babysitting his youngest sister Beth's hellions so she and her husband could have a getaway weekend at the coast, but he wasn't about to tell Weston that. Playing uncle to three kids under the age of eight had worn him out more completely than a two-day partying binge in Atlantic City. When he'd called his mother to grumble how tough it was, she'd had little sympathy.

"You were twice as challenging as Beth's kids. You couldn't sit still for five minutes. Always on the go, always asking a million questions. You know all these gray hairs I have? Your fault," Louisa Mason had said. "I can't wait until you have four or five boys of your own, the spitting image of you."

"Mom, that's just evil." He'd chuckled.

Sam smiled at Weston, remembering his wild weekend. "Sorry, I'm not the kind of guy who kisses and tells."

"You're no fun."

"Get your jollies somewhere else. Whatcha got on the Stanhope case?"

Weston shook his head. "Not much. Scuttlebutt in MI-6 is sending an agent over from London."

"MI-6? Why are they interested?"

"Apparently MI-6 believes the Stanhope break-in could be the work of an international jewel thief they've been tracking for years. Goes by the name of Joshua Benedict."

"What about our case, *the Blueblood Burglar,* got any new leads on that?" Even though the NYPD had tried to keep the socialite party larcenies quiet, the media had gotten wind of the crimes and dubbed the thief the Blueblood Burglar. So far, there had been a total of seven robberies over the course of the past three weeks.

Sam had been asked to track down a couple of leads on the Stanhope case, so the Blueblood Burglar had had to wait.

"Hey, Mason," one of the rookies hollered down the hallway at Sam. "There's some uptown hottie at the front desk asking to see you."

Uptown hottie?

For no good reason at all Sam thought of Cass Richards.

Even though she lived in Tribeca, she looked like an

uptown hottie, with her regal air and her elegant ways. But why would Cass come here to see him at seven o'clock in the morning? He suspected she wasn't an early riser. In his experience, pampered women rarely were.

"I knew it." Weston broke into a grin and rubbed his palms together. "You've got a new woman. I havta see this."

"Weston, don't make me hose you off," Sam threatened. "Do us all a favor. Go home and make love to your wife, for crying out loud."

"That's no fun," Weston sulked, but thankfully did not follow him.

Even though Sam had immediately pictured Cass when the rookie had said "uptown hottie," he hadn't really expected her to be waiting for him at the front desk.

But there she was. Looking more beautiful than anyone had a right to look.

She was casting nervous glances around his less than glamorous work environment and carrying a book underneath her arm. Funny. He'd never have pegged her for a reader.

Several of the guys were giving her the once-over and Sam was startled by the unexpected urge to punch out their lights. Damn, what a bunch of horn dogs. Was he going to have to issue drool bibs? Then again, he could hardly blame them. Cass was serious eye candy.

She was dressed in a simple black blouse and a black and white floral skirt with a swingy hem but there was nothing simple about the way the clothes clung to her curves. She personified elegant sex appeal.

The minute she saw him, relief washed over her face. "Hi," she chirped and wriggled her cute little fingers at him.

"Hi," he said, feeling as loopy as he did when his niece Amanda gave him that gooey, big-eyed "you're-my-hero-Uncle-Sam" smile of hers.

"Woooo," one of the rookies teased. "Mason's got a girlfriend."

He snapped his head back around and glared at the rookies gathered at the front desk, shooting them his dirtiest, deadliest look usually reserved for hardened criminals.

"Roll call. Now," he barked.

Their smug grins evaporated, as did they, vanishing down the corridor like ghosts fleeing an exorcist.

"Wow," Cass said. "Impressive show of authority."

"Don't be too impressed. They're just rookies. Easily cowed."

"Ah," she said, "And here I was thinking you were the great and powerful Oz."

"If you recall, the great Oz had his bluff in on the whole of the Emerald City."

"So he did." She tilted her head and shot him a flirtatious glance.

Don't fall for it. She's a master at getting men to do her bidding.

"I'm glad you came down," he said.

"Oh?" She batted her eyelashes provocatively. "Why's that?"

Sam realized the desk sergeant was about to tip over in his chair he was trying so hard to eavesdrop. "Why don't we find a more private place to talk?"

He took her by the elbow and guided her into an empty interview room. In a totally feminine gesture, she smoothed down her hair.

"Is this where you grill criminals?" She glanced around, clearly fascinated. "Is that one of those two-way mirror thingies like you see on television cop shows?"

"Have a seat, Cass." Sam reached over and pulled out a chair for her.

"Thank you."

She plopped her delectable butt down in the chair and his hand tingled with the memory of how that butt had felt cupped against his palm.

He hauled up a chair beside her. The scent of her perfume took hold of him and refused to let go. Sam wasn't a fanciful man by nature, but his heightened olfactory sense made him more sensitive to aromas than most. Her fragrance provoked poetic comparisons. Realizing he'd made a mistake scooting up so close to her, he leaned away, trying to distance myself.

But it was no use. He was ensnared.

Cass smelled of lightning the instant it struck a purple mountain orchid. No, no. Her essence was more like the taste of crème caramel eaten with a platinum spoon. No, that wasn't right either. Her fragrance embodied the sweet melody of a lover's sated breath after a long night of excellent sex. No, that was too elemental. Her smell was lighter than that, softer.

Forget it.

There was no pinpointing her, but Cass's scent created a sharp yearning inside him. She was a sultry wind fit to keep him stark awake and plotting midnight indiscretions.

"Listen," they said in unison and then both gave a nervous laugh.

"You go," she said.

"No, no, ladies first."

He didn't mind letting her start. He wasn't looking forward to breaking the news that she was considered a person of interest in the Blueblood Burglaries. Her name was the only one that had appeared on all seven guest lists and it had been his reason for going to see her last Friday.

"Okay." She placed her book on the table.

The binding had cracked and it smelled old, moldy. She flipped the brittle yellowed leaves open to a page bookmarked by a folded piece of newsprint. The book was in French.

When Cass unfolded the sheaf of newspaper article and he saw the photograph of the White Star, his cop instincts prodded uneasily. Something was fishy here, but he wasn't sure what.

Cass tapped a long slender painted fingernail against the illustration in the book. "Look at this."

Sam looked. The photograph of the White Star

amulet stolen from the Stanhope auction house three days earlier identically matched the drawing in the French text.

His uneasiness escalated. Why had she come down here to show him this? Until that precise moment he hadn't considered that the break-in at the auction house was even remotely related to the house-party thefts. The modus operandi in the two cases was very different. But now, he had to wonder.

"Where did you get this book?"

Pink lips parted, her pearly whites flashed provocatively. "My sister just bought an antique store in Connecticut and this weekend I was helping her unpack some boxes. We found this book inside. We'd read about the robbery at the Stanhope and I thought maybe the book might have some bearing on your case."

Sam sent her a long, assessing glance. His instincts told him that it was no coincidence that she'd shown up here with this particular book and the article, especially when she was already a possible suspect in seven other jewel heists.

But again, his logic found no clear connection between the two cases, nor could he reconcile why Cass would sashay into the police station and throw more suspicion on herself.

Unless she wanted to get caught.

And then there was his damnable heart that didn't want to believe anything bad about her.

"So what do you think? Does it help?" Face tipped up to his, she leaned in closer.

"Hard to say." *Play it cool. She's trouble, Mason.* "Do you mind if I keep the book, have some other people look it over?"

"Oh no, not at all." Earnestness perked her blue eyes. He reached for the book, but she put her hand over his to stop him before he could pull it away. "There's just one catch."

Wasn't there always?

"Catch?"

"You've got to promise to keep me informed about your progress in the case. I love mysteries and legends and stolen artifacts and exciting stuff like that."

A lightbulb switched on in his brain. Sam understood the real reason she'd come down here to show him the book and he hardened his heart against her bedazzling smile.

God, but she was ballsy. What a cool customer. Strolling in here, flashing that sly grin, batting those baby blues, offering up the book—which wasn't enough to prove or disprove anything, but it was enough to whet his interest—simply so she could find out what the police knew about the thefts.

She must think he was the dumbest cop ever to lumber on the face of the earth.

Okay, fine, he would oblige her curiosity. On his own terms. He could string her along, give her just enough information to hang herself.

He would turn this around to his advantage. He'd been trying to figure out a way to finagle an invitation to one of the most anticipated social events of the year.

If the thief was going to strike again, he or she was bound to do it at Bunnie Bernaldo's party.

He'd done his research and learned Bunnie's father had made his fortune importing French cheese before he and his wife had been killed in the crash of their private plane. Bunnie had inherited millions. In the ensuing years since their death, the Bernaldos' only child had become famous for her extravagant taste in jewelry, her cutting-edge parties and her laxness with personal security.

A jewel thief's trifecta.

Sam had also done his research on Cass. On the surface, she seemed innocent enough. She'd been born twenty-nine years ago to James and Victoria Richards from Brookline, Massachusetts. The second of two daughters, making her the baby of the family. Normal childhood. She had lots of friends and even more acquaintances and never seemed to miss whatever good time was going on around her. Fun-loving and likeable, she had a penchant for living beyond her means.

And that was what concerned him most.

"You've got your stipulations," he said, placing his other hand on top of hers. "I've got mine."

Their gazes locked. The air crackled with tension.

"Yes?" She sat up straighter, her eyes brighter and her smile wider, playing the game.

If he hadn't been so pissed off at being manipulated he would have admired her spunk. "You work at Isaac Vincent. I'm assuming that you know Bunnie Bernaldo personally."

Bunnie, Sam had discovered in the course of his investigation, had bought herself a job as a fashion columnist for *Moment* magazine, the trendiest fashion rag in print.

"Of course I know Bunnie. She and I were at Vassar together, although she was a couple of semesters ahead of me. Why?"

Sam had a sudden idea. And he would execute it on his own time so he wouldn't have to run it by the brass, but he had to play it just right.

Think on your feet. Keep your head in the game.

"Let's just say the NYPD considers Bunnie a person of interest." He threw the idea out there, not sure where it had come from, with no guess as to how to use it. He was simply going to see if she'd take the bait.

He'd only get one shot at this.

"In the Stanhope robbery? No way!"

"You don't think she's capable?"

Cass waved a hand. "Are you kidding? Bunnie likes the limelight too much for a clandestine career as an auction house bandit. Besides she's loaded. She has no reason to steal."

"It might not be Bunnie herself, but someone within her sphere of influence." *Like you.*

"Could it be her boyfriend, Trevor Moon?" Cass whispered. "I've never liked that guy. Smarmy. It's him, isn't it?"

Sam shrugged, gave her a noncommittal look.

"Right," she said. "You're not at liberty to divulge that much information."

He nodded. "So do you think you could rangle me an introduction?"

"I can do so much better than that," Cass said, glee dancing like sunshine in her blue eyes. "How would you like to go to *the* event of the season?"

"And that would be?"

"A weekend party at Bunnie's house in the Hamptons this Friday night."

"Ms. Richards," Sam said, "you've got a date."

4

SAM WAS JUST A REGULAR GUY, born and raised in Queens, New York. He'd never had a good excuse to venture out to Long Island and he was feeling decidedly fish-out-of-waterish. What if he embarrassed Cass by eating with the wrong fork or mispronouncing foie gras or spitting out the damned foie gras into a ten-dollar linen napkin if it tasted as gross as it sounded?

Maybe he'd get lucky and Bunnie Bernaldo wouldn't serve foie gras.

Why the hell are you worrying about this stuff? You're here to catch a jewel thief. Who cares about impressing a bunch of snobby socialites?

He didn't care about snobby socialites. What he cared about was how he'd look in Cass's eyes, and that was a dangerous thing, especially if she turned out to be the thief.

He told himself that his fascination with her stemmed from having touched her bare butt. If he hadn't touched her bare butt he wouldn't be this enchanted.

Ah, there was the rub. He had touched it. Soft and round and malleable. He hardened, remembering.

Stop thinking about her butt!

That was just it. He couldn't stop thinking about her butt. Or those big blue eyes. Or that flirtatious smile. Or her evocative scent.

He was in serious trouble here.

Sam had dressed carefully for the party, choosing navy blue slacks and a black polo shirt. He didn't own any dress shoes—having thrown away the pair by some fancy-schmancy shoe designer that his ex-wife had given him years ago—and opted for the black Doc Martens half boots he wore to work. He packed his overnight bag with similar clothing for the remainder of the weekend, leaving his holey Levis and Hard Rock Café T-shirts at home. He'd thought he'd done well.

Until Cass opened her front door and gave him a quick once-over. To her credit, she quickly hid her disappointment, but for a split second he spotted the oh-my-God-he's-got-the-fashion-sense-of-a-serial-killer look in her eyes. He's seen that same disappointed expression before, on Keeley's face.

Cass looked like something straight out of a fashion magazine. She wore a sea-green dress that put him in mind of a Grecian goddess and gold-and-green-striped pointy-toed shoes that looked as if they must be pinching the blood out of her feet, but she didn't seem to care.

Her cleavage was on full display and he liked what he saw. Draped around her slender, swanlike neck was the scarf she'd gone out on the ledge for and she'd twisted her hair up off her shoulders, anchoring it in place with a sparkly hair clip.

He stared at her, unable to believe he was escorting this gorgeous babe. *You're not escorting her, you're investigating her. Never forget that.*

Her apartment was just as sophisticated as she. Sleek European-style furniture. Simple tasteful designs. Understated, elegant colors. Funky modern artwork on her walls. Way over his head and his budget.

He tried to imagine her in his living room with his brown plaid couch and his coffee table with the wood worn smooth where he propped up his feet and his plasma screen TV he'd spent too much money on, but admitted it was worth every penny during football season.

It was a vision too incongruous to conjure.

"Nice place," he said.

"Thank you."

"Do you live here alone?"

"No." She shook her head. "I couldn't afford this place by myself. My roommate, Elle, is an actress and she just left on the road for four months with the touring company of *Mamma Mia.* I'm thinking about taking on a temporary roomie in the meantime. If you know anybody who's looking for a short-term housing solution, send them my way. I could sorely use the cash."

Sam wasn't paying much attention to what she was saying because he was too busy letting his gaze rove over her long lean legs. "You look great. Really, really great."

"Why, thank you." She smiled coyly. "The dress is Alberta Ferretti."

"That's an expensive fashion designer?"

"Right."

"How do you afford clothes like that on an associate public relations specialist's salary?"

"How did you know that I'm a PR specialist?"

"Detective. I detect."

"Well, Detective." She pressed a delicate forefinger against her full, glossy red lips. "Shh, don't tell anyone, but I get a big discount."

The five-fingered discount? Sam wondered and his stomach soured.

"The next Jitney leaves in half an hour," she said, turning her wrist over to consult her watch. "We could catch the subway to 86th Street. It would be faster than a taxi in Friday evening traffic."

"We don't have to take the Jitney. I have a car."

"You have a car?" She looked impressed. At least he'd gotten that right.

"Actually, it's my cousin's. Don't get your hopes up. Nothing fancy."

"A car is a car and we won't have to drag our overnight bags with us on the subway."

An hour and a half later, after Sam—fibbing up a blue streak—filled her in on his supposed investigation of Bunnie and Trevor, they arrived in the picturesque town of Southampton.

He felt bad for lying to her, but there was no other way around it. If he'd told her the truth, she wouldn't have brought him to the party. Then he felt stupid for feeling bad. If he caught her stealing, then she was a criminal and he had no reason to feel remorse. If she wasn't the thief, no harm, no foul and she should understand he'd simply been doing his job.

"How do we get to Bunnie's mansion from here?" Sam asked as he turned off the main road and headed toward the beach.

"We're too early," Cass fretted. "I had no idea you'd get us here so quickly. Drive around a while."

"We're right on schedule," Sam argued, tapping the clock in the dash of his cousin Manny's 1998 Toyota Camry. Amid the BMWs and Mercedes and Porches cruising the streets, Manny's sensible family car was definitely outclassed. Maybe they would have been better off to have taken the Jitney.

"Long Island schedule is different from Manhattan schedule."

"The party starts at eight and it's seven fifty-nine."

"You've never heard of being fashionably late?" She arched an eyebrow.

"My mother taught me it was rude to keep people waiting."

"Trust me on this. Only dorks arrive early."

"Hey, if dorks are punctual, then okay, I'm a dork. What you see is what you get. I like being on time."

"It's official, then. You're a dork."

He grinned. "Would you wear an I Heart Dorks T-shirt if I bought you one?"

She looked as if he'd suggested she sell her soul to Satan.

"Just joking," he mumbled.

"I might wear one to bed," she conceded.

Great. Now she thought she had hurt his feelings and she was trying to smooth things over by throwing him crumbs.

When embarrassed by a woman, do what any red-blooded man would do. Knock her off balance before she realizes what a dork you really are.

"If you were going to bed with me, sweetheart, you'd be buck naked." He winked brazenly even though he felt anything but bold around her at the moment.

Cass was on her toes and she volleyed right back. "I take it you're not a fan of leather and chains?"

"Everything has its place." He tracked his gaze over her impish mouth. "But I'm an old-fashioned guy at heart. Me, my woman, soft music, candlelight, champagne. Do it right and there's no need for parlor tricks or fantasy role-playing or sex toys."

"And I suppose you know how to do it right?" She lowered her lashes, exuding a simmering sensuality that lit his pilot light.

Anything he could say at this point would sound pretty lame. He'd started this mess. How was he going to get out of it?

Sam didn't know what demon possessed him, but he pulled over, stopped the car and turned in his seat to stare at her. He tipped his head, studying the shapely curve of her cheek, the creaminess of her skin. Hair escaped sexily from her clip, long blond tendrils curling down the nape of her neck, a beautiful tempestuous creature.

His eyes narrowed at the hollow of her throat, the blue vein of her pulse fluttering beneath pale, fine skin.

Her pupils darkened, growing wider. She was like something from his hottest wet dream.

His gaze fixed on her mouth.

Cass gulped and nervously pulled at the knot of her scarf.

He leaned in so close he could almost taste her.

She moistened her lips with the tip of her perky pink tongue and his body hardened in response. It was all he could do not to kiss her.

His heart thundered and Sam answered her question at last. "With a woman like you," he said in a deep, flirty tone, "what man could go wrong?"

Immediately, Cass dropped her gaze to her lap. Nervously, she ran her fingers over the skirt of her dress, smoothing it out when it didn't need smoothing.

Had she seen in his eyes the depth of the hunger cleaving through him, the craving for her that strained his self-control? He couldn't believe the way she made him feel. He was having trouble reconciling his suspicions with his desire for her. What was it about him? Why was he so attracted to bad girls?

"Um…" she said and he noticed her hand was trembling. "Maybe we could go ahead and go on to the party."

He rattled her. Good. Now she had a small inkling into how much she affected him.

He might be out of his element, but he realized to his surprise, so was she.

It was a bit early in the season for an outdoor party, but Bunnie Bernaldo prided herself on being unconventional. Which was one of the reasons her parties were so well attended. Visitors couldn't wait to see what outrageous stunt Bunnie would pull next.

To ward off the spring chill rolling in off the Atlantic ocean, Bunnie had had workmen bring giant heaters in and place them strategically around her massive back-yard patio. She even had the cabanas open for those brave-hearted souls willing to risk pneumonia for a dip in her heated pool.

By the time Cass and Sam arrived, the party was gearing up. People spilling out into the yard, car after car arriving, dance music playing. Cass was still dis-concerted from the weird thing that had happened be-tween them in the car.

She wasn't even sure what *had* happened.

When Sam pulled over, she thought he was going to kiss her. She had wanted him to kiss her. And then he'd looked at her like she was the most precious thing he'd ever seen.

And she'd just lost it.

Her glibness totally deserted her. And she knew with-out a shadow of a doubt that he'd meant what he said.

With a woman like you, what man could go wrong?

The line terrified her because it had felt so damned good to hear. To know she could affect a man to the point where he thought he could do no wrong.

She didn't want that kind of power. What she wanted was a stiff drink and a few light-hearted laughs.

"Would you like a drink?" Sam asked, eerily read-ing her mind.

"Thanks," she said, giving him her brightest PR smile. "Amaretto and ginger ale."

"Gotcha covered." Sam went off in search of the bar and Cass let out a sigh of relief.

Thank heavens. Maybe now with him out of her personal space she could collect herself and find a way to keep him out from under her skin.

Yeah, good luck with that.

She fidgeted with the scarf. She'd doubled knotted the thing when she was in the car with Sam and it was too tight but if she kept it in a single knot, it would slip off the way it had the day when she'd leaned out the window to wave goodbye to Marissa. The day she'd met Sam.

"Cass, Cass Richards," someone called her name.

She turned to see Julia Covington heading toward her. Julia was a gem specialist who worked for the Metropolitan Museum of Art. Julia was a debutante, but she'd never bought into the social scene and Cass was surprised to see her at Bunnie's bash.

"Hi, Julia," she greeted her warmly.

"That scarf looks like it's giving you fits."

"I've tied it wrong." Cass untied it and decided to let it just hang loosely around her neck.

"Hermès?"

Cass grinned. "What else?"

"Highway robbery, the prices they charge."

"But it's gorgeous."

She didn't answer, but Cass could tell by the look in Julia's sensible dark eyes she wouldn't put up with an expensive scarf that wouldn't behave, no matter how gorgeous it might be. She stirred her drink with a green swizzle stick. "Is Bunnie putting you up for the weekend?"

Cass nodded. "You?"

"No." Julia cast a sly glance across the room. She gave her sleek hair a casual toss, clearly flirting with the man standing in the doorway assessing her with cool dark eyes. "I've made other arrangements."

"Oh?" Cass tilted her head for a better look. The guy was fall-down-dead handsome, but the minute he realized Cass was watching him, he ducked into the crowd. "Is he a new boyfriend?"

"No." Julia's patrician smile said I've-got-a-delicious-secret.

Cass leaned in. "A lusty fling?"

"Something like that."

"You lucky dog."

"Don't try to kid me, I saw your date. You're looking pretty lucky yourself. Although I must say he doesn't seem like your usual type."

"What do you mean?"

"He's rugged, earthy. You're generally on the arm of a charming playboy."

"Oh, Sam's not my date." She didn't want Julia getting the wrong idea.

"That's a shame because I thought you two looked really cute together. And if you had kids, wow. They'd be knockouts."

Kids? She and Sam? Not hardly.

"He's a detective," Cass said impulsively. She had no idea why she said it, other than to disrupt Julia's commentary on their compatibility.

"A police detective or a P.I.?"

"A police detective." Cass lowered her voice. "But I'm trusting you not to tell anyone. He's here because he thinks Bunnie's boyfriend might somehow be involved in the theft of the White Star from Stanhope's auction house."

"Really?" Julia splayed a hand over her heart. "I'd be curious to see the amulet. I heard a vague rumor about it years ago. From what I recall, the piece doesn't have much monetary value but there are collectors who want it for the ancient lore."

"Oh?" Cass dropped her voice. "What do you know about the White Star?"

But before Julia could elaborate, Sam was back with Cass's drink. She introduced them and prayed Julia wouldn't bring up the theft again, thereby revealing how indiscreet she'd been.

Thankfully, Julia caught her vibes. "Oops, someone I have to speak to is waving at me. See you later, Cass. Nice to meet you, Sam. Don't do anything I won't do." She gave them a backward wave and headed for the crowd clustered near the swimming pool.

"She seems nice," Sam said.

"She is."

"So when do I get to meet the famous Bunnie Bernaldo?" he asked.

"Let me see if I can find our hostess."

Cass took him by the hand and led him through the fashionably dressed throng. "Anyone seen Bunnie?"

"I think she went inside," said a fashion model who called herself Mystique, whom Cass knew from Isaac Vincent's. "She said something about unveiling the big party game soon."

People tittered with interest, anticipating Bunnie's surprise. For the first time since arriving at the party, Cass realized none of her married friends were in attendance. As she glanced around at the guests it dawned on her everyone at the party was single.

Very interesting.

"Remember Bunnie's survivor party where she had the guests vote each others' clothes off until everyone was running around in their skivvies?" Mystique said.

"What about the time she invited local politicians to a lavish charity dinner and seated them with their wives on one side and their mistresses on the other? I recollect there were several high-profile divorces following that one," someone else put in.

"No, no, the best one was the truth or dare Botox party. No one in Long Island could frown for three months afterwards."

Sam pulled Cass back and whispered in her ear. "What in the hell did we get ourselves into?"

She shrugged. "With Bunnie, there's no telling. That's the fun of her parties. She's rich enough and wild enough to pull almost anything."

They went into the house, accompanied by sounds of Coldplay coming from all directions.

"Bunnie?" she asked the group hanging out in the kitchen.

Someone pointed upstairs.

Her hand interlaced with Sam's, she guided him through the living room, but then stopped so quickly he plowed into her back.

"What is it?" Sam asked.

Cass ducked behind a pedestal displaying a fat bronze Buddha with a huge jade stone in his navel.

"Oh, God." She groaned. "It's Marcos."

"Who's Marcos?"

"This guy I dated for a month and I just broke up with him three weeks ago. Clingy as Saran wrap. Pray he doesn't see me."

"Cassandra," Marcos called across the foyer to her. "I'd hoped to see you here."

"Crap, he saw me."

As usual, Marcos was overdressed in a tuxedo and looking better manicured than the White House lawn. He flashed a toothy, don-the-sunshades-someone's-had-Zoom-treatment, pure white smile.

Cass whirled around and looked at Sam, who was a little rumpled and a lot mismatched, and had perfectly normal ivory-colored teeth and she realized she'd never seen a more adorable sight. She took him by the belt loops and looked him squarely in the eye.

"Kiss me, Sam. Kiss me quick and make it good."

5

THERE WAS NOTHING ON EARTH Sam wanted more than to crush his lips to Cass's, but this was coming out of left field. Suspiciously, he wondered if she was playing him for a fool, using him to make this Marcos character jealous.

Her blue eyes pleaded. "I'll make it up to you somehow. Please, just kiss me. The only thing that's going to deter this guy is if he thinks I'm really, really with you."

Sam's thoughts clashed, did heated battle with each other.

Kiss her.

Don't kiss her.

It would be wrong.

But it would feel so right.

She's a suspect.

She's also a woman.

"Please." She pressed her palms together in supplication.

"Well," Sam said, enjoying having the upper hand, "if it means that much to you."

"Just kiss me."

He took her in his arms. It had been a long time since he'd kissed a woman. He was out of practice. More from laziness than anything else. He'd been busy with his work, busy with his family and for the past year or so hadn't even bothered looking for female companionship. He really hadn't felt much of an urge. But with Cass held tightly in his arms, he was definitely feeling the urge, his body telling him that he was long overdue.

Cass's scent, the sultry smell of a storm hours before it was coming, damaged his sense of right and wrong. He craved the fragrance of her beyond all reason, like an addiction to an exotic drug. Lowering his head, he gently ran his tongue along her lips. There was something incredibly elemental in her breath—as of fire, ocean and wind.

She pulsed, buoyant and desirable. Her lips parted, inviting him in.

And for the first time in eons, Sam Mason came fully alive.

He took her mouth. Took it fierce, took it long and he did not care if anyone saw. In fact, he wanted them to see, wanted them to know that *she* was with *him*. He branded her, hot and hard.

Sam feared for a moment that in the excitement of his newfound liberation, he'd gone too far, crossed over some invisible line. But she did not shirk from his passion. Instead she met his fire with an equally compelling blaze of her own.

He plowed his fingers through her hair, pulling her closer, knocking out the hair clip, paying no heed as it hit the stone tile floor. He saw nothing, heard nothing, tasted nothing, felt nothing, and smelled nothing except Cass.

Bending her backward in his arms, he deepened the kiss.

For so long, he'd done what everyone expected of him. He'd been a protective big brother, a playful uncle, a dedicated cop. He hadn't minded. He liked pleasing the people in his life. He had dinner with his parents every Sunday. He worked hard. He was a team player. He didn't rock the boat.

And that had been fine.

Until now.

Until Cass.

He'd been sleepwalking through his life and he'd never even guessed. He'd resisted being affected by his experiences. He'd disengaged from intense impulses, tuned out powerful emotions, minimized the importance of his desires.

And now, with just one kiss, everything he'd accepted about himself was knocked askew. Maybe he wasn't affable, steady, patient Sam. Maybe a lion lurked beneath his calm exterior. All he knew was that something had started to shift inside him and it had everything to do with Cass Richards.

The piquant sting as she eagerly nipped his bottom lip with her teeth brought him back down to earth.

He pulled back, his eyes hooked on hers. "How was that?" he whispered.

"You," she said, "deserve a promotion for going above and beyond the call of duty."

He straightened with her in his arms. They looked up to see Marcos standing in front of them, a starving orphan gazing through the window of a five-star restaurant salivating over the delicious delicacies he yearned to taste, but never would.

"Cass," Marcos said.

"Marcos, hi." She beamed at him, her lips swollen from the kiss. "Have you met my boyfriend, Sam Mason?"

"No." Marcos forced a smile and extended a smooth, manicured hand to Sam. "How do you do."

Sam nodded stiffly, shook his hand. He noted that Marcos seemed to shift under his scrutiny. The man's cologne gave off a damp papery smell like a box long buried under loamy soil.

"Cass, darling, did I just hear you say you have a new boyfriend?" A petite, bouncy woman in her late twenties, who was a dead ringer for a young Bette Midler, gave Cass a one-armed hug, her other hand occupied with what appeared to be a dirty martini, although Sam couldn't have said for sure. He was more of a Michelob man himself.

"Bunnie!" Cass air kissed their hostess. "You look fabulous."

"Don't I just." Bunnie pirouetted, dirty martini sloshing from her glass as she spun, a short, stocky tipsy ballerina. "This is a very-of-the-moment grape tulip skirt by Alexander McQueen."

"It makes you look so skinny."

"You lie, but thank you. Aren't you going to introduce me to this incredible hunk of man?" Bunnie asked, stepping closer to peer at Sam and pushing a wounded-looking Marcos aside.

She raked her gaze over Sam's biceps, made a growling noise and licked her chops.

Sam resisted the urge to turn tail and bolt. He was here for a reason. Best keep that in mind. After the kiss with Cass, his mind was scattered like a fragmented hard drive. He'd need time to defrag and figure out what had just happened. But thanks to Bunnie and Marcos, he wasn't going to get it.

He did the next best thing. He blocked out Marcos, who was staring menacingly at him and he didn't dare meet Cass's gaze. He focused his mind on his job, staring at the cluster of diamonds at Bunnie's throat, taking note of their size and shape and number.

Just in case the necklace turned up missing.

"It's a delight to meet you, Sam." Bunnie offered him her hand like she wanted him to kiss it. Not knowing what else to do, Sam took her hand and lightly pressed it to his lips.

"The delight is all mine," he said, stealing a line from some movie he'd seen where the people were all wealthy and the men were all suave, sophisticated and devil-may-care. Come to think of it, Keeley had made him watch that movie so he would "know how to act in discreet company." Well, Bunnie might be rich, but Sam suspected she didn't have a discreet bone in her body.

"Aren't you the most adorable thing?" Bunnie glanced over her shoulder at Cass. "Now, this one's a keeper."

Marcos, who was still hanging around, glowered at that comment.

"Let's get this party started." Bunnie crooked a finger at them. "Come with me."

Everyone in the vicinity followed Bunnie as if she'd started a conga line. The group snaked its way through the living room to the kitchen and on through French doors leading to the patio, where most of the guests had congregated.

Cass and Sam brought up the rear. Bunnie climbed up on the redwood picnic table and everyone gathered around.

"This is the moment you've been waiting for," Bunnie said. "Finding out what the rest of the weekend has in store."

The crowd murmured speculatively.

"If you don't want to play, then buh-bye." Bunnie waggled her fingers. "This weekend is for serious gamers only. So if you're staying, look around and pick your party companion."

Sam paused, uncertain as to what this odd development would mean for his investigation. Cass was his prime suspect. He couldn't afford to start liking her too much. Maybe he should get out now while the getting was good, before something worrisome happened.

Cass slipped her arm through his, anchoring him in place. He might as well stay, ride out his doubts and see this thing through to the end.

"Everyone got a partner?"

"Yes!" came the unified answer.

"Trevor, would you do the honors."

Collective heads turned as a ferret-faced, pale-skinned man in a dark suit and a purple silk shirt unbuttoned too low, came through the crowd carrying a cardboard box. He stopped, set the box down and began pulling out handcuffs.

Titillated gasps and excited murmurs rippled through the group.

Some people headed for the door, shaking their heads and laughing at Bunnie's antics, but a good number stayed. Including Marcos. He hooked up with a slender blond model type who resembled Cass.

Trevor set about linking partners together while Bunnie's smile widened. The sound of handcuffs snapping around wrists rang out in the cool night air.

"You're going to face a series of mental, physical and emotional challenges while handcuffed to each other. You will stay handcuffed for the duration of the weekend. You'll be eating and sleeping together, so if you want out of your pair bond, now's the time to bail. But before you make your decision whether to stay or go, perhaps I should mention the first-place prize." Bunnie paused for dramatic effect.

The crowd waited.

"A fifty-thousand-dollar donation to the charity of your choice and a mention in my column."

"How do you know who wins?" Marcos asked.

"Whichever couple completes the challenges and is still talking to each other after the competition will be the victor."

Cutthroat. Bunnie Bernaldo was a master manipulator who got off on her own power.

Cass looked over at Sam. Her eyes asked, *Do you want out?*

Do you?

Cass shrugged. *I'm game if you are.*

Any other time, any other place, with any other woman, Sam would have pulled the plug. He could find another way to catch the jewel thief.

But to his surprise, Sam realized he wanted to play this game. He wanted to be with Cass and he wanted to test their budding relationship.

And he wanted to win that fifty-thousand-dollar prize so he could donate it to the paraplegic foundation that had once helped his family.

Besides, if Cass was handcuffed to him, if she was the thief, there would be no opportunity for her to steal Bunnie's gems.

"I'm in," he said.

And with that, Sam Mason committed himself to a walk on the wild side.

TREVOR CLAMPED the cool metal handcuff around Cass's right wrist, shackling her intimately to Sam. Grinning, he slipped the key into the slit at the top of a metal lock box tucked under his arm.

"That's it," Trevor said. "Game on. You're committed until Sunday morning, come what may."

Immediately, Cass freaked.

She didn't show her fear on the outside. She was too

good at public relations for that. She knew where her bread was buttered. Winning this contest would not only put much money in the coffers of her favorite charity, Suited for You, a group that gave business suits and makeovers to women of modest means who were applying for higher-paying jobs, but would also garner her a mention in *Moment*.

Free advertising. No sweeter words to a PR special-ist's ears, but in spite of the rewards Bunnie dangled, in spite of the fact Cass was interested in getting to know Sam better—specifically after that soul-stealing kiss he'd laid on her in the foyer with the fat Buddha statue smiling his approval—she couldn't help feeling like a coyote in a trap. She wondered curiously how long it would take to gnaw off her hand.

Look at the bright side. You could be chained to Mar-cos.

Over her dead body.

"Wait a minute, wait a minute," she said, snagging hold of the hem of Trevor's jacket before he could move away. "I need to go to the ladies' room."

"So go."

Cass angled her head at Sam. "With him attached to me?"

"Part of the game."

"It's kind of private, don't you think?"

"You'll find a way."

"Seriously, unlock me for a sec, Trevor."

"Can't." He seemed far too pleased to break this news to her. "Key will stay locked in the box until Sunday morning. Once it's in here—" he patted the metal box tucked under his arm "—that's where it'll stay until the competition is over."

"You're kidding, right?"

"Bunnie's rules. Only Bunnie can change them."

Meaning Bunnie ruled. And whatever Bunnie wanted, Bunnie got.

Okay, fine. It was only for a day and a half. Cass could handle this. She plastered a bright smile on her face, belying the firestorm in her stomach.

Sam stood to her right, assessing her without comment, gauging her reaction. She could see it in the set of his shoulders, the tilt of his head, the slight narrowing of his dusty gray eyes. As if he was waiting for her to unravel.

Hmph. This was definitely the downside of hanging out with a cop. They were always searching for the truth underneath the surface.

Fingers tickled lightly at her left shoulder. Cass turned her head and saw Julia, unfettered by handcuffs. Beyond Julia, standing beside the backyard gate, was her mystery man.

"Just want to say goodnight, Cass."

"You and your…um…fellow aren't staying?"

Julia lowered her voice. "Are you nuts? Alex and I are not about to ruin a perfectly great sexual relationship with Bunnie Bernaldo's forced proximity."

"Yeah." Cass couldn't help glancing over at Sam. He looked bemused by her conversation.

Already this handcuff thing was inconvenient. So much for secrets.

"You have a nice weekend." Julia used her thumb and pinkie finger to simulate a phone and held it up to her ear. *Call me later,* she mouthed silently, then said, "Bye, Sam."

He raised a hand.

Julia and her paramour disappeared.

"Looks like everyone that's participating is set," Bunnie called from her perch atop the picnic table. "How many pairs do we have, Trevor?"

"Twelve."

"Perfect. An even dozen."

Feeling antsy about her quickly diminishing options, Cass darted her gaze around the crowd. From out of nowhere she had an urge to buy something. To go shopping until this heavy feeling inside dissipated.

She shifted her eyes back to Bunnie, saw her necklace hanging awry. "Excuse me, Bun. But you're about to lose your diamonds."

Bunnie's hand went to her throat. "Darned clasp keeps coming loose." She took the necklace off and handed it to Trevor.

"Be careful, Bunnie. The Blueblood Burglar could be lurking!" one partier shouted.

Everyone including Bunnie laughed. "I know each of you here except Cass's new beau. And I'm certain he wouldn't burgle me, would you, Sam?"

"Of course not," he said.

"See, if a stranger won't steal from me, I know my

best friends won't." Bunnie cast a meaningful glance at her guests.

"Tell us about the challenges," the skinny blonde with Marcos called out.

"Yes." Bunnie cleared her throat. "For your first challenge you're to get to know as much about your partner as possible before morning. At breakfast, you'll be asked ten questions about each other. The pair who answers the most questions correctly wins the challenge. For those of you who are already lovers don't assume you have an edge. Just because you have sex with someone doesn't mean you know them. And these questions are very intimate indeed. Share your deepest fears, your darkest secrets, the most personal details of your life and you'll be the winner."

Her announcement sent fresh panic shooting through Cass. She couldn't do this. She could not get undressed in front of Sam. She could not use the bathroom in front of him. But most of all, she could not tell him her deepest, darkest secrets.

This simply wasn't going to work. She wanted out.

Her chest heaved and her breath came out in ragged little puffs. She was almost as scared as she had been on that window ledge.

Think about the money for those women who need nice clothes, not to mention the confidence, to get better jobs to support their families. Think about getting written up in *Moment*.

Screw all that. She wasn't doing this.

As if sensing her panic, Sam leaned over, pressed his mouth against her ear and whispered, "Don't worry. I have a plan."

6

"TELL ME HOW YOU LOST your virginity," Cass said to Sam.

"Do you really think Bunnie will ask that question?"

"That one's a given. She's fascinated by lost virginity stories."

"Do you want the real story, or the one we're going to concoct for Bunnie's puerile curiosity?"

"Whatever suits you." She wanted to hear the real story of his first sexual experience, but didn't think it was fair of her to ask since she wasn't willing to reciprocate.

"We could tell each other some true stuff and some false stuff and then don't say which is which. It'll make things more interesting for us, trying to guess the truth," he suggested.

Hmm, it was an intriguing idea. She would like to know some real things about him, she just didn't want to tip her own hand.

Bunnie had put them up in a beach bungalow and while the room was a bit on the drafty side this time of year, the fact that they were away from the main house and out from under Bunnie's direct supervision was a plus.

Cass lay on her belly in the middle of the bed, knees and elbows bent, feet in the air, chin propped in her up-turned palms. She had a pen and legal pad in front of her, ready to take notes.

The handcuffs lay open on the nightstand. She was glad Sam carried a handcuff-lock-picking tool and knew how to use it.

He sat across from the bed, his arms spanning the back of the love seat, an ankle cocked over one knee, looking as if he was the king of the world.

At that moment, in her eyes, he was.

He'd outfoxed Bunnie and that was no small feat.

"Her name was Natalie Nash," he said, sitting up straighter, dropping his leg to the floor. "She was eighteen, I was seventeen."

"Ah, the *older* woman. Let me just jot this down. Exactly where did this cherry-popping assignation take place?"

"We were both counselors at Camp Wonamunga."

"In the Catskills?"

"You've been there?" Sam's voice perked up. Obviously he had mistaken her for some kind of secret wilderness girl.

"Are you kidding?" she said. "This is as rustic as I get. No sleeping on the ground or going without a shower for me, thank you very much. I'm not a huge fan of wild critters or crawly things."

"You've never been camping?"

"Once. And once was more than enough. My father

took us. It was a nightmare. We had to go to the bath-room in this little building that stunk to high heaven."

"It's called an outhouse."

"I lost my prettiest pair of sandals in a mud bog. Dad forced me and my sister Morgan to go fishing. Ugh. And I got so many mosquito bites it looked like I had the measles."

"I love camping," he said wistfully. "Love getting out of the city and breathing that clean mountain air. My two sisters love it as well."

"Okay I'm the weird one because I don't like clean, fresh air and spiders and snakes. Back to your story." She tapped the pen against her notepad. "How did you do the deed?"

"Missionary position on the folding table at the camp Laundromat at two o'clock in the morning after getting thrashed on cheap strawberry wine."

"There's no such thing as expensive strawberry wine," she pointed out.

"My tastes weren't so sophisticated then." He chuckled. "I guess not much has changed. I still don't know chardonnay from rosé."

"One's white, the other's red."

"See what'd I tell you? I'm hopeless when it comes to being stylish and urbane."

"Is that a warning?"

"A promise. You don't do camping. I don't do wine tasting."

"Duly noted."

His gaze met hers. There was so much that went unspoken, but in his eyes she saw his thoughts. *You're filet mignon, I'm baloney. You're the Eiffel Tower, I'm the windmill on a minature golf course. You're a sleek thoroughbred, I'm a Shetland pony.*

She had a sudden overwhelming urge to fling herself into his arms and tell him that she loved baloney sandwiches and minigolf and Shetland ponies. And that her favorite movie of all time was *Lady and the Tramp*.

"Do you ever feel like you're two different people?" she asked, not even knowing she was going to ask it. She felt stupid for doing so and then didn't know how to get out of the question without making a big deal of it.

"Hey, don't look at me like that. I'm not crazy. I mean do you ever feel like you're traveling down one road when you're supposed to be on a totally different path and you don't know where you took the wrong turn or how to get back to where you're supposed to be? Or even if that other path exists?"

"You're talking parallel universes?"

"No, nothing that woo-woo." She waved a hand. "Forget it. I'm not making any sense."

"I sort of know what you mean," he said. "Like you've drifted off course and if you hadn't drifted you might be a completely different person."

"Not drifting," she said. "I don't drift. I move. I plot. I grabbed the wrong brass ring."

He looked at her with such compassion, she felt confused. Had he misunderstood her? Did he think she was pathetic? She shook her head, anxious to dispel any misconceptions she might have given him.

"I'm babbling," she said. "Making no sense. Too much Amaretto and ginger ale."

"So what about you?" he asked. "Tell me about *your* first time?"

Briefly she thought about telling him the truth. That it had been a quick, slightly painful experience when she was sixteen that had left her thinking, *What's the big hairy deal?* She'd done it with the captain of the swim team on the pool table in his parents' rec room and he told the whole locker room about it the next day.

But that was so clichéd, Cass decided to class up the story.

"My first lover was Russian pianist man. He took me to the Augusta Hotel in Boston where we spent the weekend dining on room service caviar and French champagne. He taught me the ways of love, composed a steamy torch song for me and gifted me with a diamond necklace to remember him by."

"Wow," Sam said. He looked taken aback. "You were stylish, urbane and sophisticated from the get-go."

"Uh-huh," she fibbed but she could no longer look him in the eyes.

"What other questions do you think Bunnie will ask?"

"You can just figure it will be something embarrassing and sexual."

"Like have you ever done it in a public place?"

"Yes."

"Have you?"

Cass smiled. "Yes and after your laundry room story we know you have, too."

"Okay, I've got one."

"Fire away."

"Ever had a one-night stand?"

"No," she answered honestly. "You?"

"Twice and I felt badly about it both times. I'm just not a one-night stand kind of guy."

"No?"

He shrugged. "It just feels too selfish."

"Oh. Ever get anyone pregnant?"

"No. You ever been pregnant?"

"Had a scare once, but everything turned out all right. Ever had a venereal disease?"

"No."

"Me neither."

"In fact, in case it should come up, my doctor recommends regular STD and HIV testing as part of a routine annual physical for sexually active singles. I'm clean as a whistle with the papers to prove it."

"My doctor too. Clean as a whistle as well. You ever been married?"

"Are we still telling the truth here?" His eyes burned into hers.

Seconds went by, their gazes locked on one another.

"It's up to you."

"Yeah, I was married once. When I was twenty-three. Lasted nine months."

"What happened?"

"She woke up one day, realized I was never going to be Donald Trump and left. You?"

"Never married."

"Ever come close."

"Nope."

"Ever wanted to come close?"

"I've never given it much thought."

"Come on, a woman nearing thirty, biological clock's ticking, you have to have thought about it."

She didn't know why, but Cass didn't like the direction this conversation had taken. She sat up. "I'm pretty tired. I'm going to get ready for bed."

"Sure, sure." He sprang to his feet. "I think I'll go for a walk on the beach, clear my head and give you some privacy."

"Just don't let Bunnie or Trevor catch you. We'll be disqualified for taking off the handcuffs."

"I'll be invisible." He went out the front door, she scurried into the bathroom.

It was only after she'd showered, brushed her teeth, rubbed down her skin with pear-scented body lotion and dressed in silk emerald-green pajamas that Cass realized they hadn't discussed sleeping arrangements. There was only one bed in the one-room bungalow.

One bed and that tiny, cramped little love seat.

Cass groaned. The only positive side she could see in the whole arrangement is that at least they weren't still handcuffed together like the rest of the poor, miserable guests.

Except the rest of the guests were probably enjoying being chained to their partners.

Cautiously, she opened the bathroom door and peered out. Sam wasn't back yet. Breathing a sigh of relief, she shut off the overhead light, but left the one on in the bathroom and the door slightly ajar so Sam wouldn't whack his shins on something in the dark when he came in. She scampered to the bed, dove under the covers and shut her eyes tight.

Why had she told Sam all that weird stuff about feeling like she was leading an alternate life? She hadn't even known she'd felt that way until she started talking. She thought she was perfectly happy. More than happy. Delirious in fact.

Obviously, she wasn't.

But when and where had these feelings come from? Was it the discussion she'd had with Morgan last Sunday? Was it a lurking feeling that she just didn't have what it took to be a wife and mother so she kept telling herself she never wanted any of those things? She wasn't good with serious stuff. She flaked out when things got hairy. Like when Nikki, her best friend from high school, got sick.

She thought about it a minute, then decided there was nothing to worry about. She got up then and painted her toenails a lovely color of turquoise.

And she immediately felt better about life.

Tomorrow, she'd make sure Sam understood she'd just been teasing. The last thing she wanted was to have that man feeling sorry for her.

WALKING BACK UP THE BEACH path to Bunnie's mansion, Sam's head was filled with thoughts of Cass.

I want her. I want her. I want her.

His blood pulsed out the beat of his desire, pushing restlessly against his veins. Just being near her made him feel restless and edgy and by nature he was not a restless, edgy man. He didn't know what to do with these emotions or the adrenaline whirling inside him.

I want to make love to her. I want to hold her. I want to know her. I want to understand her.

He raised the wrist that had been 'shackled to hers, pressed it to the back of his nose, torturing himself with the smell of her fragrance mingling saucily with his own.

Princess Oil of Olay meets Detective Sergeant Lifebuoy.

It wasn't a bad aroma.

Intriguing actually. A blossoming yellow daffodil floating on an ocean of wheat-brown sandalwood.

He thought of Cass back there in the bungalow, in the shower, running a bar of soap over her wet naked skin. She was a beauty. If fun-loving, fast-living party girls were your type.

Cass engulfed the world in an irresistible embrace, in gestures of both self-love and largesse. Sam admired her ability, liked getting caught up in the swoon of her nirvana. But maybe Cass wasn't quite the fun-loving, fast-living party girl she pretended to be. The odd question she'd asked him was still bouncing around in his head as he tried to figure her out.

You ever feel like you're two different people?

Like a thief and an upstanding citizen? he wondered.

If he'd been able to tell her the truth, he would have answered yes. At times like these, when he was setting up a suspect or going undercover, masquerading as someone or something he wasn't in order to achieve his goal. Lying was occasionally part of his job and he didn't like the subterfuge, no matter how necessary.

He strode through the back gate and into Bunnie's yard. The grounds were still strewn with party debris, empty champagne bottles, crumpled napkins, leftover food. Bunnie was sitting at the picnic table waiting for him. He smelled her cigarette before he saw the small orange glow in the darkness.

Menthol. Virginia Slims.

"Wanna drink?" She hoisted the martini pitcher and an extra glass.

Sam shook his head and seated himself across from her. The thought of a drink was tempting. Alcohol would make this meeting go down easier. But he was here to cement Bunnie's cooperation in his sting—and put some much needed distance between himself and Cass—not to make things easier for him.

"Suit yourself." Bunnie shrugged and topped off her glass.

"I want to thank you, Ms. Bernaldo, for so generously helping out with my investigation."

She shrugged. "I was having the party anyway. Your changes to my game plan were small and easy to incorporate."

He only hoped this didn't backfire on him. He hadn't gone through the proper channels or gotten approval from his boss. When Cass had stopped by the precinct with that old French book, she'd dropped the opportunity in his lap and he'd seized it.

It was unusual for Sam to gamble like this. He was a team player. But while his superiors certainly wanted him to solve the Blueblood Burglar case, wealthy people having their expensive jewelry stolen didn't qualify for his full attention or the outlay of additional departmental funds.

He was here alone. With no backup and one small gun. Just him and his cop's determination. Was it enough?

"You really think Cass is the Blueblood Burglar?" Bunnie asked.

"Just following the leads."

"She's a good person. Generous, kind-hearted, a lot of fun."

"Fun people commit crimes, too."

"You like her, don't you?" Bunnie took a long drag off her cigarette.

He nodded.

"Tough break. Having a crush on your suspect."

"Did you check your valuables?" he asked, ignoring her comment.

"So far so good."

"Let's hope things stay that way. You ready for tomorrow?"

She patted her pocket. He heard paper crinkle. "Got your list."

"Good." He stood. "I better get back. In case Cass comes looking for me."

"Sam?"

"Yeah?"

"I hope you're wrong about her."

Sam met her gaze. "So do I, Bunnic. So do I."

WHEN SAM CAME IN thirty minutes later Cass pretended to be dead asleep.

"Cass? You awake?"

She didn't answer. *Coward.*

She felt the mattress sag as he sat down on the edge of the bed. Cautiously, she opened her eyes a slit and peered at him. He was leaning over, his face cloaked in shadows as he unlaced his gawdawful Doc Marten boots.

He turned his head toward her.

Quickly, she shut her eyes. She heard the boots hit the floor, plunk, plunk. Heard him breathing.

Was he watching her? It felt as if he was watching her. She wasn't sure if she liked the idea of him watching her when she couldn't watch him back.

So open your eyes.

Nothing doing. She didn't want to be the one to have to sleep on the love seat. *Coward, coward.*

He got off the bed. The mattress sprang back up. She heard the erotic sound of his belt slithering softly through the loops as he took it off. This time she did open her eyes.

His face was turned away from her, the light from the bathroom falling across his bare back. He had already taken off his shirt and slung it over the love seat. His chest was magnificent. Lots of sit-ups had gone into sculpting those abs.

Involuntarily, she licked her lips.

He stretched fully, like an animal, powerful and elemental. Even in the darkness, her face flushed hot. She felt feverish, adrift in some delirious dream.

Her body hummed as she watched him. Her senses buzzed as the room seemed to grow smaller and smaller and he seemed to grow bigger and bigger. She was damp and sticky and oh so achy.

He tugged off his pants and then shucked off his underwear. Cass squeezed her eyes shut again, unable to handle the intensity of his nakedness, but not before she caught a glimpse of his firm, lean-muscled thighs and tight butt.

A shiver shot through her.

Did he know she was awake?

He came back and slid between the sheets without stopping to put on a pair of briefs. He was buck naked in bed with her.

She froze, tensed. Not knowing what to do. She wanted to get more comfortable but was afraid to move around. Was he going to reach for her? Were they going to make love?

A minute passed. Then two. Then ten.

Was he just going to fall asleep? The thought disappointed her.

Although it was a stupid thing to do under the circumstances, she let herself think about kissing him. His mouth crimson-hot on hers, his hands splayed flat against her spine as he leaned her backward.

She tossed, turned, closed her eyes and then opened

them to stare at the digital clock glowing ghostly orange from the nightstand.

An hour had passed.

"Can't sleep?" His voice was an electrical jolt, intense and jarring.

"No. You either?"

"I'm talking to you, aren't I?"

"Oooh, sarcasm. Learned that on the mean streets, didja, detective?"

"Anyone ever tell you that you had a sassy mouth?"

"Only men who wanted to kiss me. You want to kiss me, Sam?"

"What do you think?" He almost growled.

"So why don't you?"

He turned in the bed and his leg brushed lightly against hers. All the air rushed right out of her lungs. But then he didn't move again, or speak.

Don't forget to breathe. Take a long slow deep breath in. Let it out nice and even. The hairs on her arm rose in anticipation. She waited. Still, he said nothing. *I don't care that he's not answering me. No big deal. Maybe I misread his signals.* He got into bed naked. What was there to misread?

"I don't want to start something I can't finish," he said. Just when she was beginning to think he might have lapsed into a coma.

"What do you mean by that?"

"I'm ready for a relationship. I get the definite impression you're leery of anything long term."

"You're naked," she pointed out. "If you're really

looking for long term then why didn't you put some underwear on?"

"I always sleep naked."

"You could have made an exception this time, if you really didn't want anything to happen."

"Do you want something to happen?"

"I have to tell you, Sam, this is the lamest seduction anyone's ever tried on me."

"I'm not trying to seduce you."

"That's really good because it's not working."

"You horny yet?"

"Hell, yes."

"Good," he said. "I've got you right where I want you. Sweet dreams."

7

AT BREAKFAST THE NEXT MORNING, Sam and Cass aced Bunnie's ten questions. Their success didn't stem so much from the mostly fictitious answers they'd conspired on the night before—Bunnie asked only the virginity one from their list—but from reading each other's body language.

The sexual tension sparking between them was so intense it must have made them simpatico. Sam had no other explanation for their victory, particularly since he hadn't slept a wink last night.

He'd lain there in the darkness, listening to her soft breathing, wrestling between his desire to reach over, pull her into his arms and make red-hot love to her until dawn and his inborn need to take things slow and get it right before acting on an impulse.

Except now he was so hot for her, he'd lost all perspective. He kept forgetting he was here as a police detective and kept getting caught up in Bunnie Bernaldo's dramatic little game and the effect it was having on his sexual feelings for Cass. He'd never in his life been so inclined to ignore his conscience and pursue a woman.

"I'm going in for the orange juice," Cass said.

They'd arrived at the big house to find the massive dining room table laden with a sumptuous morning feast. Scrambled eggs and bacon and sausages and Belgian waffles and hash browns with biscuits and gravy. Filling their plates at the buffet line had been a tricky maneuver with the handcuffs and a couple of strips of bacon ended up on the floor as casualties. And after a mishap with the salt shaker, they'd learn to forewarn each other when they were about to move their conjoined hands.

"Gotcha."

Cass reached for the glass, taking his hand along with her, and when her wrist brushed against his, Sam felt the burn up his arm, into his shoulder and clear on down to lodge in his heart.

For the first time, he noticed that her firm, determined chin was too small for the rest of her face and that her nose had a tiny hump in the bridge. Her forehead was flat as a cookie sheet and her bottom lip was almost twice the size of the top. Taken feature by feature her parts were not those of a great beauty, but together those features merged in a symmetry that robbed a man's breath.

"And now," Bunnie said after applauding Cass and Sam for winning the first round, "for your second challenge."

All eyes turned to Bunnie.

This morning their hostess was awash in jewels. A diamond watch, a ruby necklace that matched her smart red designer track suit, ruby earrings and the topper was a diamond and ruby tiara.

A little early in the day for the tiara, Sam thought, but Bunnie was undoubtedly the Queen of Southampton. She was intentionally putting her jewels on flagrant display, daring the Blueblood Burglar to strike.

Bunnie opened the Bergdorf-Goodman bag that had been sitting on the table beside her and began pulling out silk scarves. Red, blue, green, purple. Every color in the rainbow and then some.

"Ta-da," she said, and looked around the table at her twenty-four guests.

Everyone waited for an explanation. Sam marveled at Bunnie's ability to capture an audience. She'd missed her calling. She should have gone to Hollywood.

"Blindfolds." Bunnie picked up a handful of scarves. "Trevor and I will come around and blindfold you all."

The people at the table looked at each other, shared meaningful glances, raised eyebrows in speculation.

"Then," Bunnie continued, "each couple will be driven, still handcuffed and blindfolded, to a location where your driver will give you a treasure map. At that point and not a minute before, you may remove your blindfolds."

"What will we be looking for?" Marcos's partner asked.

"Your quest is a replica of the White Star amulet stolen from Stanhope auction house last Friday."

This last bit about the White Star had been Sam's idea. Bunnie had loved it and commissioned her jeweler to make copies for the party game.

"The White Star represents true love. Find it and make your way back here while remaining handcuffed together. The first couple who returns with the White Star and is still speaking to each other wins. The catch? You must surrender your wallets, cell phones, beepers, watches and PDAs."

The crowd rebelled.

"No way am I giving up my wallet," one lady argued. "It's Kate Spade."

"Bunnie, you must be joking."

"There's eccentric fun and then there's downright insanity."

"It's just too *Amazing Race.* Besides, I'm not dressed for this."

Bunnie raised a hand. "You will put your valuables in my safe. They will be itemized and accounted for. I'll be fully responsible. If at this point you want out of the game, I understand. But remember, there's fifty thousand dollars up for grabs. Charity of your choice and an article about you in *Moment.*"

"We want out," one couple exclaimed. Apparently the offer of charitable donations and magazine celebrity weren't enough to offset the inconvenience of handcuffs and blindfolds and surrendering their valuables.

"Us too," said another.

And then there were ten, Sam thought and swung his gaze to Marcos and his partner, who looked staunchly committed to the game.

Cass leaned over to whisper to Sam, her hair grazing against his cheek. "Do you want to leave?"

"No way," he said, praying she wouldn't insist they go. "You?"

But he needn't have worried. Cass was the ultimate party girl.

She smiled. "Let's win this puppy."

"WALK."

"Excuse me?" Cass said.

The darned blindfold was on so tight she was seeing red and yellow starbursts behind her eyelids. After three hours in the backseat of a car with a driver who wouldn't talk to them, she was beginning to regret staying in Bunnie's silly game.

"Start walking," the driver said. "Instructions from Ms. Bernaldo."

"This has all the earmarks of a mob hit," she joked.

"Just walk," the driver said.

"Which direction?"

"Straight ahead."

"We're walking," Sam said and squeezed Cass's hand reassuringly.

She shouldn't be nervous. Nothing to be nervous about. Parlor game.

"It is nerve-racking," Sam whispered. "Not being about to see where you're going."

Her feet left the asphalt for soft earth. Where in the heck were they? Interesting development, the whole grass thing. Were they back in the city? In Central Park?

Cass tilted her head, listening. She felt a cool breeze on her face. Heard some birds chirping but no other

Central Park noises like taxi horns blaring in the distance or runners pounding the sidewalks or the noise of children at play.

Basically, she heard nothing except the wind through the trees, Sam's breathing and the sound of their shoes crunching twigs and pebbles and leafs.

Her sense of hearing heightened, as did her sense of smell. Was that pine and wood smoke?

Where were they?

The driver made them walk for another five minutes, which was no fun blindfolded, wearing handcuffs and in three-inch ankle strap heels. One wrong step and she would sprain her ankle.

"You can stop now," the driver said.

They stopped.

"Count to a hundred before you take the blindfolds off. Start counting."

"One," Cassie said. "Two."

She heard the sound of running feet and immediately yanked the blindfold off. Her intention was to see which direction the driver took off in, but she was so startled by where she was that she forgot to see where he went.

"Oh. My. God."

"What?" Sam asked.

She whipped her head around, saw that he still had his blindfold on. "Take your blindfold off."

"The driver said to count to one hundred first."

"Do you always do what you're told? Take the blindfold off."

Sam did, looked around and broke into a grin. "What do you know. We're in the Catskills."

They were standing on a gently sloping hill, surrounded by trees and mountains, with a view of a lake below them. Thick trees, big mountains and a lake that was probably filled with fish and mosquitoes—*ick*.

"I don't frickin' believe Bunnie dumped me in this wilderness," Cass ranted.

"I'm here, too."

"Yeah, but you like it here."

"It's nice, quiet."

"I'm wearing three-inch ankle strap Manolo Blahniks," she said.

"I tried to get you to change shoes."

"The other pair I brought with me were four-inchers. Believe it or not, this pair was better suited for walking."

"If you say so."

"Where's the map? The driver was supposed to leave us a treasure map."

"Look around—maybe he dropped it."

"How are we going to get back?"

"Relax. One thing at a time. First we find the amulet."

"We have no money, no cell phone. We're handcuffed together."

"You're not relaxing."

"Okay, Zen guru, wanna tell me how to go about doing that?"

"Breathe in the adventure. I thought you were Miss Grab-Life-By-the-Throat risk taker."

"Yeah, risk not getting a table at Chez Danielle's because I waited too long to make a reservation, not risking life and limb trying to get off a mountain."

"Try it, you might like it."

"You're entirely too optimistic about this."

"Look, Bunnie isn't going to jeopardize her guests' safety. I'm sure the guy who dumped us off is waiting down the road a bit in case we run into trouble."

"Obviously, you don't know Bunnie. I bet this is because she's still mad at me for stealing her boyfriend when we were in college."

"You stole her boyfriend?"

"She didn't like him anyway. With good reason, it turned out. Toby was a Mama's boy."

"I don't need to hear any more about that, thank you very much."

"Jealous?" She tilted her head back and slanted him a speculative glance.

"You want me to say yes?" He had this fierce look on his face that tickled her.

"Not unless you are."

"I don't like thinking about you in bed with other men. Does that make me jealous?"

"But you don't mind thinking about me being in bed with you?"

"Mind? Cass, in case you haven't figured out, thinking about having you in my bed has become mandatory."

"Really?" She was pleased to receive this bit of information. "I was in your bed last night and nothing happened."

"Look," he said, changing the subject, "there's the treasure map, tacked to that pine tree."

He started over to the tree and she had to follow. He took the map down, studied it, and then passed it over to her. "Looks like one of those amusement park 'you-are-here' maps. Should be easy enough to follow."

"Hey, Houdini, get out your lock-picking do-hickey and undo us." Cass held up her wrist.

"Can't. Lock-picking tool was in my wallet, which Trevor took from me after breakfast."

"You think it's kind of weird that Bunnie and Trevor are your suspects in the Stanhope break-in and they're having us look for the White Star?"

"Definitely weird," he said, but then changed the subject on her again. "I think this way is north."

"You'll end up looking pretty bad in front of the NYPD if Bunnie and Trevor steal everyone's belongings while we're out on this wild-goose chase."

"Thanks for bringing that up. But Bunnie has a reputation to uphold. I don't see her doing that." Stuffing the map in his back pocket, he headed toward a trail snaking through the woods.

Cass minced along beside him. "They could hire someone to break in and steal the valuables."

"Yes," he said. "They could, but if Bunnie's involved in the heist at Stanhope's why draw attention to herself with petty larceny?"

"Marcos's watch alone is worth sixteen grand. I was with him when he bought it. That's hardly petty."

"In comparison to the haul from the Zander estate,

it's peanuts. Besides, Bunnie's worth millions, why bother with small potatoes?"

"Properly invested small potatoes can grow into big spuds. Or so my brother-in-law, the investment banker, keeps telling me."

"Smart man."

"Do you play the stock market?"

"I have a nest egg. You?"

Cass looked down at her shoes. "These babies are my investment. I figure invest in looking good and everything else will take care of itself."

"Translation, you're totally broke."

"Yes, but I'm spending the weekend in the Hamptons with the possibility of earning fifty grand, eating rich food and sleeping in a beachside bungalow and it's not costing me a red cent."

She stumbled over a log and her knees crumpled but Sam pulled her upright with the handcuff. "Thank you."

"But look at you. You're handcuffed to a man you barely know in the woods which you hate and you had to spend the three-hour drive getting here blindfolded. You've paid for it with your dignity."

"Hey, I'm not here by myself. Who's handcuffed to me?"

"Besides," Sam said. "It's twenty-five grand."

"What is?"

"You only get twenty-five grand. I get the other half. And the money goes to your charity not you."

"But I get mentioned in *Moment* magazine. Do you have any idea how many free lunches I'll get out of that?" She tripped again, lumbering clumsily against him, but he didn't seem to mind.

"Your investments are costing you big time. I think it's time to sell." He stopped.

The look in his eyes did not bode well for her Manolo Blahniks. She tried to keep going, getting as far away from him as her tether would allow—which was only about five inches.

He went down on one knee.

"What *are* you doing?"

"Put your foot up here." He patted his upraised knee.

She eyed him suspiciously. "Why?"

"Because I said so."

"Who died and made you king?"

"For once, could you please just do as I asked?"

"If you chop the heels off my shoes like Michael Douglas did to Kathleen Turner in *Romancing the Stone,* I'll kill you with my bare hands."

"Big threat coming from such a petite woman. In case you haven't noticed, I don't have a machete handy with which to do any heel chopping, so you can relax on that score."

"You want me to hate you? Is that it?"

"Foot on my knee. Now."

"Is this your caveman impression? Because I'm not impressed." She sank her hands on her hips and scowled at him.

"No, this is my guy-who-doesn't-want-to-be-handcuffed-to-a-woman-with-a-broken-leg impression." He patted his knee again.

Tentatively she eased her foot onto his knee. His big fingers looked incongruous as he worked to unbuckle the strap from around her ankle.

"I have to admit, you've certainly got the ankles for these shoes," he said.

"Thank you."

Sam took off one shoe, and then held out his hand for the other.

"What now?" she asked when he was finished. The ground felt cold and squishy beneath her bare feet.

"Piggy-back ride."

"How? We're handcuffed."

"You drape your right arm around my neck, come around and climb on my back."

"I'm not as skinny as I look."

"But I'm stronger than I look."

"You're sure about this?"

"Get on."

Cass climbed on his back. "What about my shoes?"

He hung them by their heels over a nearby tree branch. "We'll pick them up on the way back."

"What if someone takes them?" she fretted.

"Last time I checked, bears weren't into making the cover of *Moment* magazine."

"Touché."

"You're welcome," he said as he started down the trail once more.

"Thank you," she said, trying her best not to feel like Cinderella.

8

THIRTY MINUTES LATER Sam was wearing out. Cass wasn't heavy and he was strong, but traversing down a hill, sidestepping rocks and boulders, all the while handcuffed and trying not to drop her, wasn't as easy as it looked.

The sky had turned moody. The sun, which had already crested its zenith, played tag with the gray clouds staggering across the western horizon. Even though they'd eaten a hearty breakfast, his stomach kicked with hunger pains. He wished he'd had the foresight to stuff some of those breakfast rolls in his pocket. Unfortunately, he'd been just egotistical enough to think he'd have aced Bunnie's challenge by now. His entire plan was unraveling miserably.

Now, he only had one thing on his mind. Get that damned fake and get out of here with both him and Cass in one piece.

And the only reason he was even going after the replica was to keep up appearances for her.

Cass's soft arm was wrapped around his neck and her cute little face was resting against his cheek and she smelled like a combination of pine forest and prima donna and the scent drove him wild. Her breath was warm against the back of his neck and her sturdy but slender legs were strapped tightly around his waist.

Okay, make that two things on his mind.

Even though he was trying his best to focus on the present moment, he kept getting jarred back into last night when they'd shared a bed.

But nothing happened.

Maybe not on the surface, but something had happened, no doubt. Something a lot more intangible than sex, but significant nonetheless.

He'd been daring her to come across that bed after him, baiting her with his nudity and he had no idea why he'd done it. Had he been testing her? Had she passed? Or failed? What was wrong with him? If he'd wanted her, why hadn't he made the first move? Why had he solidly lobbed the ball in her court? Why had he hesitated?

Because making love to Cass was wrong and not just because she was a robbery suspect. Even if she was innocent, he was not. He'd set her up, used her. But the problems ran deeper than that. They were from two different worlds. She lived a champagne lifestyle and he had a beer budget. She resided in a light, airy fantasy world. He was firmly rooted in a much darker reality.

Face facts. Much as you want her, she scares the living hell out of you.

By nature he was the kind of guy who went with the flow, took things in stride, and easily meshed with his fellow man. He was unhurried, deliberate and reliable. But

Cass, with her giddy, carefree, impulsive style, disrupted his equilibrium. Being with her made him feel as if he was pushing against the force of a great rushing river, swallowed up by the sheer power of her enthusiasm.

"Your stubble is scratchy." Cass breathed against his ear and sent a hot shaft of longing bolting straight through him.

"Sorry," he mumbled. "I have a heavy beard."

"I think it's kind of hot."

What was hot was the way her legs kept rubbing up and down against his flank.

"Don't go all rich, airhead, hotel heiress on me," he growled. "You're too smart for that."

"You think I'm smart?"

"I know it."

"Most people think I'm a flighty ditz."

"You can be a flighty ditz and still be smart."

"Thank you."

"You're welcome."

"Are you bored? We could sing ninety-nine bottles of beer on the wall, if you're bored."

"Don't even."

Speaking of flighty. There she went again, off on a tangent. Bored was not one of his problems. How could he be bored with a gorgeous woman on his back?

"Okay, no singing. So what do you do for fun? When you're not being a snarly cop that is."

"I hang out with my sister's kids."

"You're an uncle? How nice. Is that fun?"

"It has its moments."

"Okay so when you're not being a cop or an uncle what do you do?"

He shrugged and the movement brought his shoulder blade into contact with her breasts. He had to close his eyes briefly and swallow in a big gulp of air to get himself under control. "I dunno. Work out at the gym."

Cass let out a sigh of exasperation. "Let's say you're not at work, your sister is out of town with her kids, it's Saturday night and you've already done your workout for the day. Now what does Sammy do? Parties, clubs, pool halls?"

"I might go to a concert."

"Really? What kind of music."

"I like jazz."

"Oh."

He could tell from the disappointed sound in her voice that she didn't like jazz and he felt as if he'd failed a very important pop quiz. "But really," he said. "I like just about any kind of music."

"Pop?"

"Sure," he lied, not knowing why he did so other than he didn't want her to think ill of him.

"Gotcha!" she said gleefully. "I hate pop. You just said you liked it because you thought I liked it."

"Yep, you got me," he said, peeved at her for leading him on. But she was right. He did have a tendency to go along with whatever the person he was with enjoyed. His opinions on trivial things didn't matter that much. He saved his battles for the big issues.

"So what else?"

"I go to baseball games occasionally."

"Mets or Yankees?"

He hesitated.

"Don't try to read me. What team do you like?"

"Well, the Yankees are the Yankees."

"So you're a Mets fan."

"Yeah," he said and smiled. He didn't often admit it.

"Good, good, we're getting somewhere. Me, I'm a Yankees fan, but not so strongly that I can't keep company with a Mets fan. So what's your passion?" she said, her heels brushing against his flank as he walked.

"Passion?"

"You know what gets you charged up? Me, I've got tons of passions. Clothes and shoes and jewelry. I adore fashion. Food—eating it that is, not cooking it. Hate to cook."

He loved listening to her chatter, her wild little monkey mind spinning excitedly, sucking him into her orbit. She was so passionate that it was easy to get lured in by her.

Be careful. You're a cop and she could very well be a thief.

Rationally, he knew this, but as a man, he felt something entirely different.

"And parties of course and games and movies and books and horses." She sucked in her breath rapturously. "I love horses but I haven't been riding in so long that it really is a sin."

"Why don't you go riding?"

"So many bright and shiny things, so little time."

"Here we are." He slogged into a dry creek bed at the bottom of the hill.

"Here we are what?"

"Where the reproduction is hidden."

Sam found a nice-sized boulder, walked over to it and helped Cass dismount from his back. They sat side by side while he rested.

"Let me see the map." She held out her hand.

He plucked the map from his back pocket and passed it over to her. Her expression turned serious as she studied it.

"According to this the amulet is supposed to be right here. So is it just lying around somewhere?" She looked over her shoulder, peeking at the ground. "Are we supposed to dig someplace?"

Sam lay back on the rock, resting his tired shoulder muscles. He put one hand up to shade his eyes.

"Nope," he said. "It's not lying around somewhere and we don't have to dig."

Her forehead knit together in a frown. "What is it then?"

He pointed up at a tree limb ten feet above them.

She lay on her back next to him and followed his gaze. From one slender branch dangled the replica amulet strung on a bright red ribbon. The faux jewelry winked in the sunlight, mocking them.

"Bunnie Bernaldo is an evil, evil witch," she said.

"On that we can agree."

"At least it's a climbable tree," she said after staring

up at it for a good five minutes. "Lots of low, strong branches."

"Let's shake it," Sam said. "See if we can knock the amulet loose."

"I'm all for the easy way."

They shook the tree. Vigorously. It was a no go.

"Looks like we're going to have to climb."

"I was afraid you were going to say that." A tree, why did it have to be a tree? Why couldn't it be water? He was a great swimmer, had no fear of that. No. It had to be a tree. And a very tall one.

"Could you boost me up to the first limb?"

"In handcuffs?" The logistics were laughable. Except he wasn't laughing.

"No. Here, let me show you what I mean."

She had him brace his back against the tree and squat in a sitting position. Then she climbed his knees like he was a chair, twisting around to accommodate the handcuffs until she'd seated herself on the bottom limb.

"Now what?"

"You come up too."

"This is ridiculous, you're going to fall."

"Don't be so negative."

"I'm not negative, just realistic."

"Realism is all well and good, but it's spirit and imagination that'll take you to the stars."

"I don't want to go to the stars," Sam grumbled. "I just want to get that thing and get out of here."

"Why are you so cranky all of a sudden?"

"I don't want to climb this damned tree."

"Come on. It'll be fun." And then she turned and started climbing higher, giving him no choice except to follow her or pull her to the ground.

The wind picked up as the sky darkened, blowing a lock of hair over his forehead. He made it to the first branch, but by then she was already on to a second one. Her bare feet were at his eye level, his left arm raised high to help facilitate her upward mobility.

Then he made the mistake of glancing at the ground. Even though they were only about three feet up, his stomach started to roil.

Don't look down.

Fair enough. He would look at her toes. That should take his mind off his fear of heights. Cute tiny toes painted up whimsically in glossy turquoise polish with little diamond heart nail jewelry embedded at the center of each big toe.

His fingers itched to reach out and stroke her elegant feet. His pulse pumped. He'd never understood foot fetishes before, but now, he did. There was something so compelling about her toes. He had a mad urge to take one of her pinkie toes into his mouth and suckle it.

He dragged in a deep breath, shocked by what was going on in his head. This was almost as dangerous as looking down.

"I'm going higher," she said. "You with me?"

Then Sam made the fatal mistake of looking up.

One glance was all it took. One look at that glorious round butt of hers, encased in a pair of lacy scarlet panties and it was over the edge. Over the limb. Tumbling backward onto the hard-packed earth.

Taking Cass with him as he fell.

SAM WASN'T BREATHING. His eyes were wide, stunned, staring at the sky.

"Are you all right? What happened?" Cass peered anxiously down at him, biting her bottom lip in concern. She'd landed astraddle his lean muscular waist, his body breaking her freefall.

He wheezed. His face was red, his lips tinged blue. He held up one finger indicating that she should give him a moment.

Poor baby, he'd had the air slammed from his lungs.

She rolled off of him, lying side by side with him on the ground, squeezing his hand tightly while she waited for him to catch his breath.

"I lost my balance," he said, once his breathing had returned to normal.

"Did I move before you were ready? We've got to figure out what it was, so we can coordinate our movements. I don't know how many times we can fall out of a tree without breaking something."

"It wasn't you."

"What was it?" Cass sat up. "Was it the wind? Did it gust hard enough to knock us out of the tree?"

"It wasn't the wind. It was me."

"You?"

"Forget the amulet. We're not going back up that tree again."

"Why not? I could have reached it. Just a few more feet."

Sam swallowed.

Cass could tell that it was costing him a lot of pride to say what he was about to say. "I'm afraid of heights."

"You? You're afraid of heights?"

"Yeah, me."

"But…but…that's impossible. You came after me on an eighth-floor ledge."

"You have no idea how much that took from me."

"Why, Sam, that makes your actions even more heroic." She turned misty-eyed and a lump of emotion hardened in her throat.

Without warning, he reached up with his unfettered hand, buried his fingers into the hair at the nape of her neck and pulled her head down to his.

Cass gasped, startled. Her stomach contracted. His actions were so passionate, so sudden, that every ion in her body sang, charged with erotic tension.

His mouth crushed hers, demanding, intense.

She was shocked by the great, unexpected force in him. His lips burned hers. A flame, bright and glowing and golden.

Danger, a challenge, the unexpected, the unknown, anxiety, fear, excitement all converged inside her to produce a wild euphoria. She felt as if she'd been given a shot of adrenaline.

The sexual guarantee embedded in that commanding kiss damaged Cass's ability to reason. Every nerve in her body was electrified. The contour of him; the rich roundness of his bottom lip, the chiseled angle of the upper, the boundary where the masculine texture blended into the damp softness of his inner mouth.

Slowly, her lips relaxed, dreamlike as a strange calmness stole over her, a foreignness that provoked her. She surrendered into the feeling, into him.

Then just as abruptly as he'd grabbed her, Sam turned her loose and pulled his mouth from hers, saying gruffly, "Don't make me out to be a hero."

He sat up, rolling as far away from her as the handcuffs would allow.

What had just happened? Tentatively, Cass fingered her bruised lips.

How unexpected. The many layers of Sam Mason. She turned and studied his face. He looked away from her and Cass realized she'd underestimated him. He was far more complex than she'd ever guessed.

Cass understood why he'd done what he'd done. It had cost him so much to confess his weakness that, desperate to hide his frailty, he'd countered with the unexpected, taking her by surprise, kissing away his embarrassment.

But no matter what he might think, his fear of heights was not his flaw. He hadn't gotten upset until she'd called him a hero. That's where his discomfiture lay, even though he would probably deny it if she pointed that out to him.

No, Sam didn't like being seen as special or different or unique from anyone else. He liked fitting in, liked being part of a team.

Unlike Cass who reveled in the limelight, he shied

from it. Seeing undo attention as a threat to his inner stability. This new knowledge of him was both striking and seductive.

Sam's vulnerability touched her deeply. He was much more mysterious than she'd ever believed. She wanted to unwrap him like the biggest present on Christmas morning, ripping off the attractive wrapping, opening up the sturdy box, ruffling through the stratum of delicate tissue paper to find the treasure buried deep inside the heart of this man.

"Stop looking at me like that," he growled.

"Like what?"

"Like you're psychoanalyzing me."

"You just can't keep doing that, you know. Leading me on, then thrusting me away."

"What are you talking about?"

"Push-pull. Push-pull. I'm tired of you yanking me around."

"I'm not yanking you around."

"The hell you're not."

"What do you mean?"

"You honestly don't see it?"

"See what?" He sounded exasperated.

"Last night, in the car, before we went into the party. You pulled over the car, acted like you were going to kiss me and then stopped with your mouth less than an inch from mine. Then later, when you got into bed with me, totally naked and didn't make a move. And now you kiss me and then just as quickly shove me away. And you don't want me psychoanalyzing you? How the hell else am I supposed to figure you out?"

"Have I really been doing that?"

"Ya-huh. If you were a woman you'd be called a cock tease, but since you're a guy I suppose that makes you a…"

"I get it."

"So what gives? Is it me? You're attracted to the naughty girl, but too clean to make a move on her?"

"No! God, no." He shoved his free hand through his hair. "I would never think that about you."

"Then why won't you just do me?"

"Here? In a public place?"

Cass glanced over her shoulder. "I don't exactly see the public lined up for a trolley ride. Besides, you lost your virginity in the laundry at Camp Wonamunga. That's a lot more public than this."

"I lied about my first time," he said. "I wanted it to sound exotic."

"Really?" She grinned. "I lied, too."

"No rich Russian pianist at the Augusta hotel in Boston?"

"Nah."

"Too bad. It was a great story."

"I'm in PR. It's sort of expected. So how did you really lose your virginity?"

"Pool table in Jenny Miller's rec room."

"Get out! Me, too. Not with Jenny Miller, of course, mine was Brad Harper."

"I've never made love outdoors," he confessed.

She clicked her tongue. "You've been sadly deprived. We need to rectify that. Now."

"I can't. I'm a cop. It's indecent exposure."

"Only if we get caught." She winked.

Clouds bunched. The wind kicked up. The air molecules quivered around them, thick with delicious anticipation and luscious innuendo. The changing weather escalated her lust, the elements pushing Cass toward something monumental. How exciting to make love with an electrical storm headed their way. How taboo. The mad rush of desire dizzied her head.

"Come on, Sam, do it. Take me right here, right now on this rock."

"It'll be rough on your back."

"Don't be so practical. Lose yourself."

"I don't want to bruise you."

"I don't care about bruises. I want you that badly. Don't you see that's what great sex is all about? Being daring, being spontaneous, wanting someone so damned much that you don't care about the inconsequential things like bruises."

"Cass." He was sweating, his eyes dark with desire. "It's not right."

"So what? Let it be wrong. Let's be wrong together."

She was risking it all. Throwing herself at him, caught up in the whirl of the weather and the moment. Her gamble twisted her stomach, knotted her shoulders with spine-tingling tension. And a real vulnerability that torqued her erotic feelings for him into overdrive.

She didn't care if she got hurt. Her passion was that

reckless, that headlong. All she wanted was to feel him inside her. She flung her arms around his neck.

"Take me, Sam. I want you."

But Cass never got to finish her seduction.

Lightning flashed. Thunder boomed.

And rain bucketed down.

9

"MY MANOLOS. They're gonna be ruined. I knew I shouldn't have let you leave them hanging in that tree."

A fork of yellow-hot lightning smacked the ground not a hundred yards away. Thunder crashed.

"Forget your damned shoes," Sam yelled, wind lashing rain into his face. "We've got to find shelter. Lightning could kill us, not to mention flash flooding."

Cass stood beside him shivering, her fair hair plastered against her skin, highlighting the faint dusting of freckles across her nose Sam had never noticed were there. Her wet sweater lay flat against her breasts, close as a second skin. Her nipples were beaded tight, with cold or arousal he didn't know which, but the sight of those puckers aroused him enormously. What an inconvenient time for an erection.

Mindful of the handcuffs, Sam bent and scooped Cass up off the rock.

"Sammy, are you happy to see me?"

"Hush, woman, and let me think."

To his amazement, she quieted.

This was a well-visited state park. There should be

other visitors, campers, park rangers, tents, outdoor restrooms, something, any kind of help or shelter. Sam turned in the direction where he believed the road might be, praying that he was correct in his assumption. He was cold, wet and already his arms were aching from carrying her, the handcuffs chafing his wrists.

Lightning snapped like a lion tamer's whip cracking behind them, exploding into a shock wave of reverberating sound. Rising heat scorched the air. His brain buzzed.

"Sam, look out!" Cass cried.

He jerked around to see the tree that they'd tried to climb cleaved in two by the arcing electrical discharge. As they watched dumbfounded, the top of the tree snapped off, the remaining naked wood jutting up like a spear.

Cass leapt off Sam's back and he pulled her clear just in the nick of time.

The severed top of the tree smacked the ground, leaves and branches smoldering in spite of the driving rain.

And at their feet landed the faux White Star amulet.

"Omigosh," Cass exclaimed, slapping a hand over her heart. "Just think if you didn't have a fear of heights or if you'd taken me up on my offer to have sex on that rock, we'd be dead right now."

THIS WAS TWICE Sam had saved her life. Once from the window ledge and now from a falling tree.

Cass clung to him, feeling guilty for being such a burden, the fake White Star on the red ribbon strung around her neck. She felt his powerful thighs move as he carried her in search of shelter and safety.

They could have easily died.

Still could, in fact. Although the lightning was moving away, the heavy rain remained. She struggled to keep her teeth from chattering. No matter how miserable she was, Sam had to feel worse.

Cresting the rise with her in his arms, he staggered and Cass feared he was going to fall, but then he tightened his grip, pulled her closer against his chest. "Look, Cass."

She turned her head. Saw a paved asphalt road and a campground. Momentarily, her spirits soared.

But the campground was empty. No tents, no trailers, no one.

Except for two gray cement buildings.

Ugh, outhouses.

Okay, so it wasn't the Waldorf, but it was shelter from the weather.

"I told you I would take care of you," he said. He looked so proud of himself. Cass was proud of him, too.

"Thank you."

When they got closer, much to Cass's happiness, only one of the buildings turned out to be bathroom facilities. The other structure was a Laundromat, complete with a large built-in table for folding clothes and vending machines. To top it off, someone had forgotten a blanket in one of the dryers. They explored, delighted with their shelter.

"Can you believe someone forgot their blanket? It's almost like fate left it behind for us to find."

"About time. I'd say fate owes us. And what have we here?" He bent and picked up something that had been wedged between two of the washing machines.

"What is it?"

Sam grinned. "A hairpin. I think I can use it to get these damned handcuffs off."

"Thank God. My wrist is raw."

"Put your wrist up here." He indicated the top of a washing machine situated directly beneath the fluorescent lighting.

For several minutes he worked on the handcuff with the hairpin and at last they were sprung free.

Cass rubbed her sore wrist while Sam dug in his pocket, found several crumpled one-dollar bills and fed them into the change machine. Quarters spilled into the change cup—ching, ching, ching.

"Slip out of your sweater and skirt and we'll dry them."

"Can't. They're dry clean only."

"Then we'll lay them out to dry."

"You're wet, too."

"So I am."

They looked at each other, the air between them sparking with sexual energy. She could smell his testosterone, knew he wanted to make love to her as much as she wanted him to, but something was holding him back. A sense of honor? His conscience? Who knew? But Cass was determined to find a way around his resistance.

"I'm telling you it's fated," she said blithely. "Free blanket, dryers, a folding table, no more handcuffs."

She got no further.

Sam had her in his embrace and he was kissing her as if he was a death row inmate with a miraculous conjugal visit just before his execution.

Ah yeah, now this was more like it. No more of that sleeping naked in the bed next to her without touching her nonsense.

Grabbing the hem of his polo shirt, she ripped it off over his head. Grabbing, she reached for his belt buckle while he unbuttoned her sweater, his damp fingers fumbling in haste. Grabbing for another kiss on the fly.

"Wait, wait, wait," she said.

"What is it?" He looked harried, frustrated.

She had to make sure he knew that this was just fun and games. Sam was a nice guy. The last thing she wanted was for him to get the wrong impression and get his heart hurt.

"You're cool with this being a casual fling, aren't you?"

He nibbled at her neck, the heat of his erection poking against his straining zipper. "Fine and dandy."

"Last night you said you were looking for a long-term relationship."

"I'll look later. After this. After you."

That should have comforted Cass, but it didn't. It wasn't because she didn't believe him, but rather it was the words "after you" that echoed so hollowly in the chamber of that empty laundry room.

And in her heart.

She didn't want anyone to come after her. How selfish and unreasonable was that?

It was the first time she'd ever felt this way. The sensation was very strange. It felt as if something in her bloodstream had been blocked up and suddenly broken loose. Like something inside her heart just popped open and flooded her body with energy and endorphins.

What was wrong with her? She wasn't a long-term kind of woman. She'd known it all her life. She liked having her own way. Having fun. Living the good life.

And wondrous, unexpected encounters like this were part of that good life. Cass closed her eyes and did what she did best. Lived in the moment. Seized the adventure and breathed it in.

Sam peeled off her wet sweater, lifted it off her shoulders and then carefully draped it over a nearby washing machine, smoothing it flat so it wouldn't wrinkle as it dried. His actions touched her, the way he took care with her clothes.

When he was finished, he straightened and came back to her, desire turning his gray eyes the color of gunpowder waiting to explode.

His big hands settled around her waist, but over the top of her skirt so he still wasn't touching her bare skin. She watched him lower his gaze and smile at the faint flush heating up her skin.

He kissed her and their hot breaths mingled, steaming up the laundry room. She nibbled his bottom lip. He groaned softly.

He unhooked her bra and once they were both bare-chested, except for the replica White Star around her neck, he shifted gears. Slowing things down even further.

Cass understood why. Even though he wanted her as desperately as she wanted him—his body told her that clearly enough—he wanted this to last. Wanted to savor the memory of their first time.

Ah, the joy of discovery.

He cupped her face in his palms, dipped his head and kissed her again with a soul-stealing, grade A, world-class kiss that curled her toes.

The moment was brilliant. He was brilliant. It was her most brilliant first time ever.

She moaned. Loving, yet hating, the sweet torture. She wriggled against him, her breasts pressed flush against his muscled chest.

He ran his fingers up and down her shoulders. She threw back her head and he trailed his kisses to the underside of her neck, nuzzling and nibbling.

Experimentally he rubbed his thumbs over her nipples and they beaded so tight they ached.

"Ah," he said. "So you like that?"

"It feels awesome."

A hazy hotness draped over her, thick with sexual urgency. She wanted him so badly that her need was a solid, unyielding mass in her throat.

"What about this?" He laved his tongue along the underside of her throat.

She shuddered against him.

"And this?" Lightly, he tickled the skin on the inside of her upper arm.

When his mouth found its way back to hers again, the laundry room disappeared and there was nothing except the tyranny of her heartbeat and the searing splendor of his taste on her tongue.

"God," he said. "I love how responsive you are. All I have to do is touch you here…" He touched her and she moaned. "And you unfurl. You make me feel like the best lover in the world. That's a precious gift, Cass. Thank you."

His praise made her blush. His appreciation exhilarated her. She'd thought she was as turned on as she could get, but she'd been wrong. The look in his eyes, the way he held her, sent her blood into a searing boil.

She arched into him, rubbed her pelvis against the front of his pants, the denim of his jeans abrading her flesh. He lifted his head, his marauding mouth going back to dominate her lips with another hungry kiss.

The force of his desire caused her to tremble and sweat. Her knees quivered. Her heart pounded.

He tunneled his fingers through her hair.

She felt his presence in every cell of her body, in every breath she took, in every strum of the blood pumping through her veins.

He was pushing her to the breaking point, pushing her over the edge of sanity, down into temporary madness. If she didn't get him, she would lose her mind.

She was going to snap in two like that lightning-struck tree if he didn't do something soon and just as she was thinking it, just as her pelvis was raw and full and aching for him, he tugged her skirt down over her hips.

And then he dropped to his knees.

"Sam," she gasped.

"Cass," he crooned.

She braced her back against the heavy commercial grade washing machine behind her. He slid one finger into the strap of her panties and slowly teased them down off her hips, over her thighs, past her calves to her ankles. She stepped out of them.

She surrendered completely, coming to him with her entire history. Vulnerable. Unprotected. Shaking in the naked revelation. Allowing herself to embark on this erotic journey with a partner whom she barely knew, a fantasy come true. Rich with chemistry and possibility.

Danger, challenge, the unexpected, the unknown excited her nervous system, delighted her soul.

"Open your legs," he whispered gently, lovingly.

She spread them.

His wet tongue teased, slowly licking her outer lips.

He buried his face in her. Inhaled her. Then caressed her with the sensuous sweep of his tongue.

Ah, there were splendid benefits to an earthy man. None of her suave, sophisticated men had been inclined to pleasure her this way.

Then he took her bottom in both his palms and lifted her up onto the washing machine until her shoulders rested against the back and her buttocks sat perched on the very edge, pelvis tilted upward.

Blindly he searched for the coins in the change machine, fed them into the washer and turned it on. She heard the gush of water, felt her own body flood in response.

Lowering his head again, he went back to pleasuring her with his sweet, inquisitive mouth until she was wet with his love.

Gently, he suckled her twitching, hooded cleft. She was wild with ecstasy. Wild for him.

Outside the storm lashed and groaned. Inside Cass trashed and moaned. She was so swollen and throbbing for him so ready and hot.

Mewling, she grabbed for his hair and held on for dear life, never dreaming anyone could make her feel this good.

He knew the way to make love to a woman, his mouth responding to a silent calling of her body.

His fingers touched and tickled and tingled. Her butt, her inner thigh. Again, he slid one finger deep inside her wetness, while his tongue continued to strum the feminine head of her.

"More, more," she cried, writhing against his tongue, her bare butt bumping against the cool metal of the washing machine. It hit the spin cycle and began to vibrate beneath her.

Lightning flashed outside the window. Thunder clapped in applause.

The vibration, the storm, the noise, Sam's red-hot mouth. It was all too much. More than she could stand.

Her orgasm was sudden and powerful, blinding in its intensity.

She cried out, rough and glorious. As she rode the crest of it, he held on and when she was finished, he helped her to sit up.

Without speaking, he took the blanket she'd found, spread it out on the laundry table, then went back to get her, laying her down gently on the table.

Drowsily, her eyes closed.

"Oh, no, sweetheart," he murmured. "No sleep for you. We're just getting started."

10

ALMOST DYING, SAM KNEW from being a cop, was one
hell of an aphrodisiac. Nearly being killed by a lightning-felled tree charged him up, just as falling off the
eighth-story window with Cass had amplified his sexual response the week before.

The musky taste of her loitered against his tongue.
Divinely sensual. Deliciously decadent. Her flavor was
as expensive as caviar and truffles, her body luminous
with the luscious perfume of rich, aromatic lust.

His body responded to her siren's call.

He toed off his shoes, shucked off his jeans and
climbed onto the table beside her.

"Turn onto your stomach," he commanded.

"What are you going to do to me?"

"Do you want me to make love to you?"

"Yes." The word was a sigh of longing on her breath.

"Then you must trust me. Turn over."

She trembled, her gaze flying to his face. "I'm afraid."

"That's what makes it so exciting."

She obeyed, tentatively rolling over until she was
lying prone in front of him.

His breath escaped in a harsh rasp as he reached out to stroke his fingertips along the supple curve of her spine until he reached the small of her back.

There it was.

The magnificent butt that had dominated his waking fantasies every single day for over a week.

His rough fingers staked over her silky flower-petal soft skin. He watched the muscles of her buttocks tense, sensing her nervous thrilled as she waited to see what he would do to her.

One lone finger went on a scouting mission, sliding down to the top of her graceful crevice. The heat of her body was hotter here.

He massaged her with the utmost care. Tenderly exploring. He found her tight little circle and barely touched her there.

She shuddered.

He brought his lips to the fleshy part of her buttocks. Kissed her and then nibbled gently, adoringly. Admiring, tasting and revering her.

"You're so beautiful," he said. "So gorgeous."

"No more," she complained. "I have to see your face. I have to kiss you." She flipped over and in her fierceness, threaded her arms around his neck and pulled him down flush against her.

They stared into each other's eyes for a long wordless moment and then they tore into each other again.

Licking, nibbling, biting, caressing.

Intoxicated on each other they staggered into bliss. They murmured dirty words, whispered sexy pillow talk. Taking them higher and higher, making themselves crazier and crazier.

Sam teased her, transporting her to the brink again, but refusing to let her spill over.

"Wait," he whispered, nibbling her earlobe.

"I must have you now."

"Not yet."

She groaned, loud and plaintive. "How much longer are you going to torture me?"

But he was torturing himself as much as he was torturing her. When he trailed his fingers so wickedly over the curve of her hip to the secret place below, his own body quivered with a rush of testosterone as she shivered beneath his touch.

The sight of her rapturous face sent his brain in a frenzy of excitement. The pressure inside him was so great, his head throbbed and his ears rang. His body's stark craving for her catapulted him into uncharted emotional territory, flying him into a sea of all-consuming desire.

He was euphoric, optimistic, rejuvenated, revitalized. He wanted it to last as much as he wanted to plunge his shaft deeply into her. It was a battle he was destined to lose.

She arched against him, begging for release from her torment. Then abruptly Cass broke their kiss. He stared at her, glassy-eyed and confused.

"Condom?" she rasped.

Condom? He couldn't even think. "No condom."

"Oh, no way!"

"Wait, wait. We've both been tested and we know we're clean. Besides I haven't been with a woman in over a year. Are you using birth control?"

"I'm on the pill," she said.

"Do you want to go ahead?"

"Yes, yes, yes."

Thank God. He'd have gone insane if he had to stop now. He pressed her back against the table, cradling her head in his palm.

What a woman.

Wrapping her legs around his waist, she thrust her pelvis up to meet his and he slid into her deep. They locked into a tempo so easy it was scary. They were new to each other and yet their bodies were intimately attuned to some ancient rhythm.

He gazed deeply into her eyes, his fingers threading through her long blond hair. Heat radiated from her body, suffusing him in warmth.

And as the heat filled his heart, a sudden stillness filled his head. He was so very aware of her, but not in the crashing thrust of lust that had thundered through him before. This was a quiet, shining sense of newness.

Cass's upturned face was bathed in the glow of the overhead light. Surreal, ethereal, perfect.

Sam liked the way she made him feel. Strong, reliable, trustworthy.

Keeley had rarely made him feel this way. With her he'd usually felt anxious and undeserving somehow. But Cass, who on the surface reminded him of his ex-wife, was in reality, nothing like her at all.

She locked her hands around his neck as he drove deeper into her. He felt the muscles in his back ripple beneath her touch as other muscles in his body, quivered and jerked. Angling his hips, he cupped his hand beneath her bottom, shifting until he found a new place to please her with his cock.

He felt the shocking elation of the unknown. As she grew more and more aware of him inside her body, moaning his name, pulling him deeper into her, his confidence faltered. This uncertainty, this vulnerability, created a new man of him. Salt of the earth, Sam Mason, fell away and in his transformation he became aware of his own strangeness inside her.

"Sam," she cried, the sound of her voice rushing over his ears like an ocean tide, sweeping them away.

Their gazes fused. Pupils widened, breaths escalating into frantic pants.

For one earthmoving flash, a jolt of comprehension of what they'd embarked on traveled between them, some unexpected soul knowledge profound and extremely essential. But before Sam could claim the feeling and identify it, they tumbled together into the abyss.

SAM NIBBLED THE NAPE of her neck, drawing Cass from sleep. She turned into him and he kissed her with such ardor, she was instantly aroused. He curled his arms around her, moonlight slanting in through the laundry-room window above their heads.

The storm must have passed while they slept.

What would it be like? Cass wondered giddily, to be

held in his arms like this every night? To be kissed with such eager abandon on a regular basis?

The thought sent a shivery thrill jolting down her spine. She'd never thought that about any man, never wanted one long term.

Did she now?

Too soon. It was far too soon to be thinking like this. Besides, nobody says he wants you for the long haul. Just drift. Just drift and enjoy.

That wasn't hard to do. Not when Sam's tongue was doing wickedly delicious things to the underside of her jaw.

They found each other's mouths, hungry, desperate. He was insatiable, but so was she.

She was sore and damp and starving for more of him.

"Take me from behind," she begged.

He flipped her over, levered his body against hers, his rock-hard shaft cradled against her buttocks. Gently, he reached around and dipped a finger into her juicy core, then slowly caressed her straining cleft.

She held her breath, waiting, trembling in anticipation, knowing that at any minute he was going to plunge his throbbing erection into willing wetness.

And then he was in her.

She gasped, shocked and delighted at how big and hard he was. He pumped, moving his hips in a circular motion that gradually turned into hard, rhythmic thrusts, all the while still stroking her maddening bud.

They shuddered and clung to each other, holding on for dear life, their abdomens stiffened, their legs stretching and their backs arching as they groaned in tandem pleasure.

Exhausted, they fell silent except for their heavy contented breathing and sigh of release. Slowly, they kissed and caressed, lingering in the afterglow.

Sam was everything she wanted him to be and so much more than she'd ever dreamed. Amazing, this man she'd found.

"Thank you," he whispered and she kissed him with gratitude because it was mutual. She was so thankful for all he had given her.

A HAPPY, SILLY LITANY of nonsense words popped spontaneously into Cass's head. *Sam, Sam. Sam I am. Sam ate Spam. Sam, Sam, Sam. Sammy. Sambo. Sambony. Sambon-i-roni. Sam-a-licious. Green Eggs and Sam. Heeere's Sammy.*

She was on her side, facing him, knees pulled to her chest, arms stacked under her head, watching him sleep. Her gaze tracked from his face down to the underside of his jaw to the muscular column of his throat to the beefcake-calendar-quality chest.

Rugged. Hard. Totally masculine. Chiseled chin. Proud nose. Beard shadow. Sculpted cheekbones. Who would ever guess he was afraid of heights?

There were black and blue marks on his arms and shoulders and the soreness in her body told her she had a few marks of her own. Were the bruises from the fall from the tree or their night of wild monkey sex?

Probably both. It was the good kind of soreness, hard fought and well earned.

The memory of their night was like a bouquet of red and white spider lilies, sweetening the air with a cinnamon and vanilla tingle, fresh and alive and vivid. Purity versus pleasure.

Sam's eyes remained closed.

Cass stared and stared and stared.

"Stop staring at me," he ordered.

"I'm not staring at you."

He opened one eye and peered at her. "Liar."

She smiled at him.

He groaned.

"Did someone wake up on the wrong side of the table this morning?"

"I can barely move," he complained.

"I've got breakfast."

"Breakfast?" The promise of food perked him right up.

"I retrieved those quarters you left in the change dispenser when we got...um...distracted from our laundry last night and I checked out the vending machine."

"What did you get?" He propped himself up on one elbow.

She reached up for the haul she'd stashed on the window ledge. "You have your choice of cheese curls or peanut butter crackers or a chocolate bar."

"I'll take the peanut butter crackers."

"Good man. You know to leave the chocolate for a woman." She passed him the crackers and happily unwrapped her chocolate bar.

"These are stale," he said, the cracker exploding into a shower of crumbs when he bit into one. "Ah, hell."

"Don't worry." She winked. "You can eat stale crackers on my table anytime."

He laughed and tweaked her nose. "I love your optimism."

"The chocolate's not bad. Wanna bite?" She pulled the crinkly foil wrapping down an inch and broke off a scored section.

"You go ahead, but toss me the cheese curls. I'll give those a try."

They munched and crunched for a few minutes. Cass leaned her head against Sam's chest, listening to the lub-dub of his heart, feeling perfectly content and sated.

"This wasn't quite how I pictured Sunday," Sam said, lazily trailing his fingers over Cass's bare breast.

"Is reality better or worse?"

Before Sam could answer, the door to the laundry swung open and a perky woman about her own age bounced in, heading straight for the dryers without looking around.

The instant Sam spotted the woman he grabbed the blanket and threw it over them, making sure Cass was covered.

The woman startled at the sound, peered over and spied them on the table looking guilty. She splayed a hand over her chest.

"Excuse me, I'm sorry, I didn't know anyone was in here. I just came for my..." Her eyes fixed on their cover. "Blanket. But I can see you need it more than I do. Just keep it." She spun on her heel and ran for the exit.

"Wait," Sam called out. "Please, wait."

The woman hesitated at the door, hand tensed on the knob, her gaze landing everywhere except on them.

"Hi," he said. "I'm Sam and this is Cass and we got caught in the storm last night and ended up here."

Cass waved at her.

The woman forced a smile. "Cate. Cate Wells."

"Nice to meet you, Cate. I'd get up, but…"

Cate looked at their clothes strewn across the laundry room and lifted a hand to shield her eyes. "I understand. That's okay."

"What we're wondering," Cass said, joining in, "is if you could give us a ride."

"Um…"

It was obvious the woman didn't want anything to do with them, but Cass could tell she was a kind-hearted person. Just when she was about to plead their case, Cate reached over and snatched the faux White Star off the washing machine.

"Oh, my gosh," she exclaimed. "Isn't this stolen?"

And then she spotted the handcuffs on the floor.

"Don't you people move," Cate said bravely in spite of the fact her chin was quivering. She swallowed hard. "I'm calling the cops."

"I AM A COP," Sam told her. "NYPD."

The woman looked like she didn't believe him.

He waved at his pants that had gotten kicked across

the laundry room. "My identification badge is in my back pocket."

Gingerly, she retrieved his pants, found his identification and then glanced back over at them again.

"Is she your prisoner?" Cate narrowed her eyes. "Are you a dirty cop making this woman perform sexual favors in exchange for a lighter sentence?"

"No, no," Sam said, completely flummoxed by getting caught naked and by Cass snickering behind her hand.

This wasn't funny. It was highly embarrassing. He was an officer of the law and he'd just broken public lewdness laws by having sex in the laundry room of a state park.

"What about this?" Cate held up the White Star.

"Look closer. It's a well-crafted fake."

Cate held the amulet up to her eye. "Oh," she said. "It is."

"Now that we have that out of the way, do you think you could give us a ride?" Sam explained what had happened and how they'd ended up in the laundry room under Cate's blanket

"Sure." Cate shrugged. "I was on my way back into the city."

Cass tugged Sam's arm. "What about my Manolos? I don't have any shoes."

"You have Manolos?" Cate's eyes lit up. "I can't afford them on my salary."

"I can't afford them either," Cass confessed. "That's why their loss is so heartbreaking. They're somewhere out in the woods, damaged by last night's storm."

"Tsk, tsk." Cate clicked her tongue. "That is so sad. What kind were they?"

"Ankle straps." Cass was misty-eyed. "They perfectly matched my dress."

"Ouch."

"I know."

Women and shoes. Sam shook his head. Something no man would ever understand.

"I have a pair of old flip-flops out in the car that I can let you have," Cate volunteered. "Just so you're not running around barefooted."

That cemented it. Cass and Cate bonded.

Cate gave them a ride in a Mini Cooper borrowed from a friend. She'd been in the Catskills communing with nature and she'd been caught by the storm. She'd ducked in the laundry room to dry out her blanket and clothes. Her friends had rescued her, but she'd accidentally left the blanket tumbling in the dryer. She'd come back that morning to retrieve it before heading home.

Cate dropped them off at the Jitney station with a wave. Sam and Cass took the bus back to Bunnie's place in Southampton. Just before they entered the mansion, Sam snapped the handcuffs back on their wrists.

They were the last guests to return.

"So much for winning the money," Cass mouthed to Sam as Trevor ushered them into the dining room, where everyone else was polishing off a lavish lunch.

"Not so fast," Bunnie said, having caught Cass's comment. "Only five of our other couples returned with their amulets. And of those five, none of them are speaking to each other."

Sam glanced around the room. Sure enough, more than half of the couples who'd been handcuffed together were no longer sitting side by side and most couldn't even look at each other.

Huh. Imagine that.

Being handcuffed together had only brought him and Cass closer. Of course they'd had their Houdini time, free of hardware, but in those moments they'd been even more intimate than when they'd had the handcuffs on.

"So you win," Bunnie said. "To what charity should I make the check out to?"

"No, Bunnie," Cass said. "We can't accept the check. Sam and I cheated. We took the handcuffs off."

Sam looked at her, surprised but heartened by her honesty. If she would tell the truth about something like that, how could she be the kind of woman who would steal jewelry from her friends?

"Thank you, Cassandra, for your candor. Since the rules specifically stated you had to remain handcuffed throughout the challenge, that means Marcos and Deirdre Johnson are the winners." Bunnie applauded and the rest of the room joined in.

"Yes!" Marcos jumped up from his chair and made a motion as if he was spiking a football in the end zone. He charged over to Cass, shoved his nose inches from hers and jeered, "In your face, Richards."

Sam stepped in front of Cass and sent Marcos an I'd-love-an-excuse-to-kick-your-high-society-ass glower. "What's that?"

"Nothing," Marcos mumbled and turned away.

But Sam wasn't going to let it go. He slapped a hand on Marcos's shoulder and spun him back around.

Marcos reflectively raised his fists.

"Apologize to Ms. Richards for behavior unbecoming a gentleman," Sam demanded. He didn't care that the entire room was watching or that Cass was plucking anxiously at his shirtsleeve. He wasn't going to let this overpriced, overstuffed snob disrespect her.

"Um, Sam," Cass stood on tiptoes to whisper in his ear. "Marcos won a national boxing championship when he was at Eton."

"Yeah?" Sam clenched his jaw and drilled his hard-edge stare right into Marcos's eyes. The wet cardboard smell of him made Sam want to sneeze. "I boxed on the streets of Queens. You want to take it outside?"

Marcos hesitated, considering the thrown gauntlet.

"Bring it on, pretty boy." Sam's voice was steel, his fists just aching to defend Cass's honor.

Marcos muttered something under his breath that Sam couldn't make out, but he backed down. He looked at Cass. "I'm sorry, Cassandra, if I disrespected you in any way. In my excitement over winning the competition I spoke out of turn. Please forgive my boorish behavior."

Sam had to admit as far as apologies went it wasn't half bad.

"I accept your apology, Marcos." Cass smiled.

"Congratulations on winning the competition. You and Deirdre earned it."

"Now that's settled," someone at the table commented, "Bunnie, open the safe and retrieve our valuables so we can go home."

Bunnie sent Sam a meaningful glance. He nodded imperceptibly. The moment of truth had arrived. Would any of the valuables be missing?

As everyone lined up for their personal items, Sam took a strategic position near the wall safe so he could supervise the proceedings without looking too obvious.

One by one the remaining guests collected their items, bid their hostess goodbye and headed out the door until only Cass and Sam were left.

Sam took her aside. He needed to get her out of earshot so he could talk to Bunnie. "Would you like to change clothes, freshen up before the trip home?"

"Sounds heavenly," Cass said.

He took her back to the bungalow, and while she was showering he called back up to the big house to speak with Bunnie privately.

"Have you checked all your jewelry?" he asked, keeping his voice low.

"Yes."

"And nothing's missing?"

"Nothing."

"You're certain."

"Yes."

Sam exhaled heavily. He didn't realize how much

he'd been sweating this until Bunnie told him nothing was MIA.

"I'm sure it was a relief, finding out Cass isn't the Blueblood Burglar."

"All it means is that she didn't have the opportunity to steal anything. It doesn't prove she's innocent. It simply means that none of your other guests are guilty."

11

"YOU'RE AN EMBARRASSMENT to bachelorhood, you know that, Mason?" Weston ragged on him the next morning when Sam shambled into the briefing room for roll call.

"What are you talking about?"

"I found out what it is that you really do on the weekend." Weston shook his head. "And here I'd been pinning all my hopes on the fact that you were shagging a different hot babe every night."

"Your fantasies have been disillusioned?"

"Yeah. You can quit faking like you're walking funny from too much sex. The jig's up. The whole precinct knows you're not getting any. My wife and I saw your sister in the supermarket last week. She said you babysit her kids on the weekends. She said you don't even have a girlfriend." Weston drew in an indignant breath. "What's wrong with you, man? You're wasting valuable time. Once some woman finally lassoes you, you'll be longing for these single days you threw away so casually."

Sam laughed, amused at his colleague's sad attitude. Beth had done him a favor, spilling his babysitting secret. "Think whatever you want, Weston. I know where I was this past weekend."

"Yeah, babysitting." The look on Weston's face was one of sad disappointment.

Sam placed a comforting hand on his shoulder. "Even the mightiest heroes have feet of clay. This is what happens when you live vicariously through someone else. For God's sake, go home and draw your wife a hot bath, make dinner for her, treat her right. Maybe then you'll have a sex life of your own and you can stop wasting your time dreaming about mine."

"Gone, all gone." Weston looked as if he'd just been told the National Football League was going on strike next season.

During roll call, Sam learned there was nothing new in the Stanhope robbery. He also learned one of his former partners, Ron Barnaby, who'd recently been shot in the line of duty, was improving and had been to the same rehab hospital that Sam's sister Janie had been in all those years ago. He made a mental note to drop by and see Ron and to make a donation to the hospital while he was at it.

After the briefing was finished, he dragged himself over to his desk. He was bruised and battered and bleary-eyed from his wild weekend but the crazy thing was, he'd never felt more alive.

He couldn't seem to stop smiling. Thirty-six hours—give or take a few—chained to Cass's lovely wrist had changed his life in unimaginable ways.

Whenever he was around her Sam saw life through her eyes. It looked fun and fresh, exciting and new. Around her, he was more alive than he'd ever been, more involved, more his true self.

And, he had absolutely no right to feel this way about her. None at all. But feel it he did.

He'd lied to Cass. Granted, it was in the course of doing his job, but he didn't feel any better about the deception. He'd behaved unprofessionally and to top it all off he wasn't any closer to knowing whether she was a thief or not than he'd been before the weekend started.

His heart told him she wasn't guilty. Weston would say, "Heart, hell—it's your gonads, boy."

But Sam was a trained police detective. You followed the evidence. Once in a while you might pay attention to your gut, but only as far as it was reasonable under the law. What you could never, ever do in the field was follow your heart.

Or for that matter, your gonads.

Your heart and your gonads would trip you up every damned time.

Stop thinking about Cass. Get to work.

But there was no escaping her. She was part of his investigation. Intricately entwined in his case.

And his mind.

Whenever he breathed, he smelled her perfume, vanilla as candy-floss on the upper layer but with a rich, sophisticated note of sassy, foreign spice underneath that drilled a hole of longing straight through his brain the minute he smelled her.

Whenever he shuttered his eyes closed, he saw her movements projected like a movie picture against the screen of his lids, lithe as a dove feather floating down from the sky, but with a steely, determined undercurrent to her walk that tweaked his stomach with an endless need to watch her sway.

Whenever he ran his tongue over his lips he tasted her kicky flavor bursting delightfully in his mouth, tangy as jalapeño salsa but with the satisfying buttery softness of fresh baked bread stroking childhood memories of warmth and comfort and home.

Whenever he pressed his palms together, he felt her smooth skin beneath his fingertips until his entire body pulsed.

Whenever he tilted his head, he heard her animated voice filled with details and humor echoing in his ears like fairy footsteps but with the dusky resonance of midnight moans raising the hairs on his forearms and drenching his collar with sweat.

He was a man consumed.

Dammit, dammit, dammit.

He pulled his palms down the length of his face. How had he let this happen?

Better question, what was he going to do about it?

Nothing. He wasn't going to do a damn thing. He wasn't going to call her. He wasn't going to drop by her apartment and see her. He wasn't going to ask Bunnie about her.

He was going to stick to the facts and keep his emotions completely out of the fray because that's what good cops did. Sam was a master at subjugating his needs for the good of the case. It gave him a sense of inner well being, a comfort zone he associated with autonomy and freedom.

At least nothing had gone missing from Bunnie's house. Some small consolation. He clung to that tenuous life preserver, made it more monumental than it was. He'd set up a sting and he hadn't caught Cass. But was that because his methodology was flawed? Or because she was sharp enough to recognize a trap when she saw one?

What if he could prove beyond a shadow of a doubt Cass was not the Blueblood Burglar?

Only way to do that was catch the real one.

And then?

Sam shook his head. Until this was settled, he wasn't pinning his hopes on the future.

His extension rang and he snagged the receiver, grateful for the distraction. "Detective Mason."

"Sam, this is Bunnie Bernaldo."

"What's up?"

"I was mistaken."

"What do you mean, mistaken?" Sam inhaled sharply.

"The jade stone. From the bronze Buddha in my foyer. It's gone."

"SOMEONE GOT LAID THIS WEEKEND," Cass's best friend Marissa teased her over an early breakfast at Havana Eva de Cuba, one of Marissa's favorite hangouts just a few blocks from her apartment.

"How did you guess?" Cass asked.

"The news had to be juicy for you to insist I meet you at this ungodly hour of the morning." Even at 6:00 a.m. with her hair pulled back in a ponytail and no makeup on Marissa looked stunning. Cass envied her friend's exotic ethnic beauty.

"I know it's early," Cass apologized. "But it's the only time that would fit into both our schedules. Thanks for meeting me. I had to talk to someone about this and Morgan would make too big a deal of it."

"Lay it on me. I'll give you my honest opinion."

"That's what I love about you, You never mince words."

Marissa stacked her hands on top of the table and leaned forward. "So tell all about Bunnie's party."

Leaving out only the most intimate details, Cass related what had happened over the weekend. When she'd finished, she bravely met Marissa's eyes and told her the truth. "Mari, I'm scared."

"Scared?" Marissa looked surprised. "What's there to be scared of? You used protection, didn't you?"

Cass waved a hand. "Don't be so literal. That's not what I'm scared of."

"So you're going to make me drag it out of you?"

"I like him."

"And that's a problem because…?"

"I like him too much."

Marissa had raised a glass of water to her lips and stopped in mid-sip, sputtering as she swallowed the wrong way. She set the water glass down and pounded against her upper chest with the flat of her palm.

"Are you all right?" Cass asked, anxiously clasping her napkin, prepared to run for help if her friend needed it.

"Fine," Marissa said, her eyes watering as her coughing fit passed. "Are you saying what I think you're saying?"

"Depends on what you think I'm saying."

"Are you falling in love with Sam?"

"Don't be absurd. I've only known him a little over a week. I'm not falling in love with him."

"But by all accounts, it's been a very intense week. Falling from a ledge together, almost getting killed by a lightning-felled tree. Being handcuffed to a person for thirty-six hours would take its toll on anyone's defenses."

"There's no toll. No toll is being taken."

"Oh, my God," Marissa exclaimed, and slapped a hand over her mouth to hide a grin. "You *are* falling in love with him."

"Shh. I am not." Cass was getting irritated. "And please stop saying that."

"Cass and Sam sitting in…"

"Don't you dare." Cass pointed a finger. "I mean it."

"What's wrong with falling in love?"

"You know me. I'm footloose and fancy free."

Marissa shrugged. "People change."

"Exactly. For instance you could change your modus operandi of picking arrogant jerks and go for a sweetie like your buddy Jamie."

Marissa glared. "Point taken. Okay. You're not falling in love with Sam. It's just an exceptionally lusty affair. Screw your brains out. Have a great time."

"Thank you. That's all I wanted you to say."

"What are friends for," Marissa asked, one eyebrow cocked, "if not to tell us what we want to hear?"

FOLLOWING HER BREAKFAST with Marissa, Cass found herself roaming the streets of New York. She didn't have to be at work until nine and she had nothing else to do but walk and think.

She wasn't falling in love with Sam. Her friend was completely off base. She liked Sam. She respected him. She appreciated the way he'd taken care of her in the wilderness. That's what she was feeling—admiration, respect and gratitude.

Not love. Certainly not love. Never love.

Never love?

It sounded so desolate. Did she honestly truly never want to fall head over heels in love? Cass bit her bottom lip and narrowly missed getting clipped by a bike messenger as she crossed Broadway, though she barely noticed.

Where had she gotten the idea that love was a bad thing? Her parents had a great marriage and even though Morgan and Adam were going through a rough patch right now, Cass felt certain they loved each other and would eventually work things out.

She had no cheating bastard boyfriends in her past who'd used her and broken her heart. In fact, if anything, she was the heartbreaker. Not that she'd ever led a guy on. She'd never pretended to be something she wasn't. Even as a child, when her other friends planned for their wedding day, Cass found herself fascinated by stories of runaway brides.

The happily-ever-after chicks were boring. You got married and your adventure was over. What tugged at her interest were those women who turned away from the traditional path and embraced a life of numerous possibilities. Katherine Hepburn and Margaret Mead and Coco Chanel. You couldn't do that if you promised forever and ever and ever to one guy.

She tried to analyze it rationally. Deep down, what did she really want out of life?

Well, what anyone else wanted, to be happy, satisfied, fulfilled. That wasn't so strange. How had it translated into a fear of a committed, loving relationship?

Maybe it had something to do with Nikki, with her guilt over what had happened with her friend, and the realization that she wasn't tough enough to hang in there when things went bad.

She wandered past an elementary school and an old childhood memory floated to mind.

Her parents had taken her to a fall carnival at Morgan's school. The air had been crisp, the leaves turning colors, the afternoon filled with limitless possibilities and fun. She'd gone on rides and played games and watched Morgan garner theatrical kudos in the school play.

And then she'd won a cake on the cakewalk.

She could still feel the excitement she'd experienced as that lucky seven-year-old. The lady coordinating the cakewalk had escorted her to the table laden with cakes.

"Pick any cake you like," the lady had said, "but you can only have one."

Cass had stared wide-eyed.

They were all so beautiful, so incredibly crafted. There was a Barbie cake and a Hello Kitty cake and a Smiley face cake. There were cakes decorated with M&M's and licorice whips and malted milk balls. There were chocolate cakes and strawberry cakes and banana cakes. There were cakes with cream cheese frosting and cakes with butter cream frosting and cakes iced with caramel and hot fudge.

Eeeny, meeny, miney, moe.

She reached for the pretty pink Barbie cake, but stopped.

"What flavor is it inside?" she'd asked the lady.

The lady looked at a printed card in front of the Barbie cake. "Yellow cake."

Cass had made a face. She liked chocolate best. She backed up and went for a triple layer chocolate cake, but it didn't have M&M's on it. She pointed to the M&M's cake, but when the lady picked it up, she shook her head.

Why couldn't there be a chocolate Barbie cake with M&M's sprinkled on top of it?

"Pick one," the coordinator insisted. "Just pick one, already. It's not that hard to do."

She'd started crying.

"Don't cry. No crying, you won. Just pick a cake."

But she couldn't.

Cass had turned and run away. Run away without her cake because she simply could not choose just one.

The memory took her breath. Was that what she was doing with men? Running away from commitment because she was afraid of making a mistake? But in her running, she was missing out on the glorious taste of cake.

What was she so afraid of?

Honestly?

She was afraid of losing her freedom, of losing her essential self in the shadow of a man. But in her fear was she also surrendering a great deal of potential joy?

Was Marissa right? Could people really change? Could she become a person who could eat Barbie cake every day for the rest of her life and love it?

Dazed, Cass stopped walking. She looked around to see where she was and was stunned to learn she was standing in front of the 39th Precinct.

Had this been her destination all along?

She wasn't quite ready to eat cake, but maybe she was ready to think about someday cutting herself a slice to see how it tasted.

But not today.

She turned to go and in her haste to get as far away from this particular piece of cake as possible, she smacked into a man hurrying down the steps.

"Oops," she said.

"Sorry." He reached out a hand to steady her.

The sound of his voice squeezed her stomach. Good grief, it was Sam. What were the odds that she'd run into him?

Well, considering she was standing in front of his place of business, probably not all that astronomical.

"Cass? What are you doing here? Did you come to see me?"

"No, oh no. I was just passing by," she said, knowing he did not believe her. She couldn't blame him. She did not believe herself.

His posture was stiff, unwelcoming. His face expressionless. Had things changed since yesterday afternoon when he'd kissed her after dropping her off at her apartment?

"Okay," she admitted. "That's a lie. I came by to see if maybe you wanted to grab some dinner tonight, my treat."

"I can't."

"Short notice, fair enough. How about tomorrow?" Was she really saying this? Cass wished for her Hermès so she could gag herself and execute the prattling.

A pained expression crossed his face and before he said the words she knew he was going to blow her off. Knew it because she'd used the same look on many a man, but none of them had ever used it on her. She'd never given them the chance.

"Look, Cass. Things got out of hand this weekend," he said. "We did things we shouldn't have done. Don't get me wrong, it was great. Way better than great, even, it's just that..."

She didn't let him finish, couldn't stand to hear him finish. She raised her palms and nodded her head. "Right, right. I understand. Not a problem. Don't think twice about it. Good times had by all. Hope you break the Stanhope case. See ya."

Then before the rock in her throat turned to tears, she spun on her heels and sprinted away from that triple layer chocolate, M&M's-sprinkled Barbie cake as fast as her feet would carry her.

IT WAS RAINING IN THE EVENING following his encounter with Cass on the precinct steps. Sam didn't go home. The thought of an empty house depressed him. Instead, he decided to drop by the rehab hospital and see his former partner, Ron Barnaby.

Sam had been thinking about Cass all day, knowing he'd handled the situation badly, wanting to call her but reasoning that it was better that he kept his distance. Especially after finding out the jade stone, valued at eighty thousand dollars, was missing from Bunnie Bernaldo's Buddha.

Every cell in his body wanted to deny the truth, but the noose kept getting tighter. He'd gone to Southampton, dusted the Buddha for prints and discovered a dozen different fingerprints on the statue, including Cass's. The more he investigated, the more she looked like the Blueblood Burglar.

The hospital looked the same as it had twenty years earlier; tall, broad, brown brick building hulking imposingly in the rain. Inside, the hallways still smelled the same; citrus scented antiseptic, bad cafeteria food and underneath something darker. The bitter odor of tragedy.

His shoulder muscles bunched under the weight of

his coat and in an instant he was transported back in time. A gangly kid, pacing the hallways while his parents waited at his sister's bedside, not knowing whether she was going to live or not.

He hated hospitals and the ugly memories that came with them. It was the reason he hadn't already been to see Ron.

Sam wandered the corridor and passed the room where Janie had once been a patient. She was fine now. She'd learned to live with her disability. She married a great guy and had bravely moved away from her family to Madison, Wisconsin, to be with him because she loved Peter more than life itself. And Peter's family had embraced her, welcoming her with open arms. They'd never treated her as if she had a handicap. Sam admired his sister's courage and he was happy she'd found her place in the world.

Suddenly, he had the eeriest sensation that someone was staring at him. He turned around but saw no one except for nurses scuttling to and fro on their mercy missions.

A few minutes later, he found Ron's room. He was heartened to see his buddy looking well, even though he was still having trouble with his speech. Ron's wife was there, as were his two kids, so Sam only stayed a few minutes and he talked about work. He could tell from the sparkle in Ron's eyes he was happy to see him, and when he left the room, Sam felt better than he had all day.

He stopped a nurse in the hallway and asked her who he should speak to about making a donation. She directed him to the public relations office and he immediately thought of Cass and his case.

Instead of taking the crowded elevator, he headed for the stairwell. He heard footsteps behind him, but initially thought nothing of it. Visiting hours at the hospital, there were a lot of people around. His mind was still on Cass.

His nose itched. The stairwell smelled like wet cardboard and pepperoni. A pizza delivery guy, carrying boxes wet from the rain was going up as Sam was coming down.

Sam stepped aside on the landing to let the pizza guy pass on through the door to the fifth floor. When Sam stopped, he noticed that the footsteps behind him stopped too.

Strange.

Turning, he then edged quietly forward on the balls of his feet back up the stairs. His head rounded the corner of the bottom of the steps that he had just descended and he spied a pair of men's black highly polished patent leather shoes.

"Excuse me," he called out. "Can I help you?"

The feet turned to run away. Sam flung himself up the stairs in hot pursuit of the fancy shoes. The man hit the stairwell door on the sixth floor before Sam could get a good look at him. Ten seconds later he burst through the door after the guy.

The elevator doors were just closing.

The nurses in the hallway turned to stare at him.

"Shh." One frowned. "This is a hospital."

"Did you see who just got in the elevator?" he asked the disapproving nurse.

She shook her head.

"Never mind." He punched the elevator button. He was probably making a much bigger deal out of this than it was. Still, he couldn't shake the feeling that someone had been following him.

Question was, why?

"SO HOW WAS BUNNIE'S PARTY?" Morgan asked, slicing tomatoes for a tossed salad.

"It was okay." Cass shredded the heart of crispy romaine lettuce.

"Okay?" Morgan put down the paring knife and swiveled around and pinned her with a look. "Bunnie's parties are never okay. They might be crass, they might be unruly, they might be fabulous fun, but they're never just okay."

Cass shrugged. "More of Bunnie's usual antics."

"Something's wrong." Morgan narrowed her eyes. "What aren't you telling me?"

"Nothing's wrong."

"Don't lie. For one thing you never come to Connecticut during the middle of the week and out of the blue, I might add. For another thing you've been exceptionally quiet ever since you arrived. Cough it up, what's wrong?"

Damn but it was inconvenient having such a perceptive older sister.

"Did you ever find out what was up with that carved box you found?" Cass asked.

"I'm not going to let you change the subject, but yes,

I did. One of my customers has a background in ancient artifacts and she believes the box could be more than a thousand years old."

"No kidding? Tell me more." Cass propped her chin in her upturned palm while sitting cross-legged on one of Morgan's chic modern barstools.

Odd that her sister, with her obvious love of antiques, would decorate her own house in a neo-classic style. Then again there was more to Morgan than met the eye. For instance no one in the family could fathom why she had quit her well-paying job in the city to buy the antique shop in Connecticut five minutes from where she lived, but no one cared what Morgan did as long as she was happy.

Morgan held up a finger. "You're not distracting me. What happened at Bunnie's party? And don't fib. You're a terrible liar. Your face turns all blotchy when you lie."

Cass touched her cheek. "Does it really?"

"Why do you think I always beat the pants off you in poker?"

"I thought it was because you were a brilliant poker player."

"Nope, you just have a bad poker face. So no monkeying around."

Cass reached for one of the carrot sticks she'd just peeled and crunched contentedly. "When's Adam going to be home?"

"He called earlier and said he couldn't make it to dinner. I'll see him when I see him." She shrugged as if she didn't care, but the gesture was too casual. Her sister was upset.

"I'm sorry, Morg."

Morgan took a deep breath and smiled tightly. "Nothing to be sorry about. Can't be helped. Business."

Cass felt so badly for her sister she started gabbing about Bunnie's party to get her mind off Adam's absence. They ate at the bar, ignoring the pretty dining room table Morgan had set with china, a floral centerpiece and candles. Then her sister surprised her by opening a bottle of wine. It was unusual for Morgan to drink during the week.

"So go on. What happened with you and Sam while you were trapped in the laundry room?" Morgan poured herself a second glass of wine.

"You know, things heated up."

"How hot?" Morgan winked.

"You're tipsy."

"That's my prerogative."

"It's Tuesday."

"So? I'm well past twenty-one. Very well past."

"Are you sure you don't want to talk about what's going on with you and Adam?"

"There's nothing going on with me and Adam. We're a boring old married couple. Regale me with stories of your single adventures."

Cass was concerned, but Morgan was her big sister and she clearly did not want to talk about what was happening between her and Adam. She launched in with a few carefully chosen details about her night with Sam.

"So when are you seeing him again?" Morgan asked after she'd finished her story.

"I'm not."

"What? You're not seeing him again? But you just said it was the best sex you've had in a long time, perhaps the best sex ever and that's a direct quote. I can't believe you're dumping him already. He holds the record for your shortest relationship ever."

"I didn't dump Sam," Cass said quietly, toying with a mushroom on her plate. "He dumped me."

"What?" Morgan sat up straighter and blinked at her. "No one's ever dumped you."

Cass clenched her jaw. She had no idea talking about it would make her feel so bad. "I really liked him a lot, you know?"

"Cass?" Morgan sobered and reached out to rub a hand along her shoulder for comfort. "Are you okay?"

"Sure, fine." She shrugged. "He's just a guy."

"A jackass if you ask me. Using my baby sister for sex and then dumping her."

"He's not a jackass and he didn't use me any more than I used him."

"You really do like him."

"Yeah, I really do."

"This is the first time you've ever had your heart broken, isn't it?"

Cass made a derisive noise. "My heart's not broken. Heavens, no. I was just hoping for some more of that great sex."

"Well, if it's not your heart, then it's just a bruised ego. Sam Mason will forever be the one who got away and that's why you're feeling blue. Your pride took a ding. No biggie. You'll bounce back."

"Yeah," Cass echoed. "I'll bounce right back, no problem."

And then she ducked her head.

Just in case her blotchy face gave her away.

12

"MAIL CALL." The kid from the mailroom dropped the morning's correspondence into Cass's box, and then disappeared down the hall.

Feeling decidedly lackluster after taking the early train in from Connecticut, Cass drained her triple latte. Her head throbbed dully and her eyes were dry. After their second helping of chicken Marsala, Adam had called again telling Morgan that he was going to miss the last train, so he was just going to get a room at the Hilton for the night.

Following that newsflash, she and Morgan had proceeded to polish off a second bottle of wine. They'd had a grand time getting plastered and trash talking the male species in general and Adam and Sam in particular. They'd bonded like they hadn't bonded in a long time.

But this morning they'd both paid for it.

Cass swallowed back three aspirins and massaged her temples. Okay. She was officially over Sam Mason. Time to tackle the day.

She reached for the stack of mail and leafed through it. Promo ops, follow-ups to previous correspondence, requests for information. Nothing interesting enough to snap her from her gloomy mood.

Then she found the package.

It was a white, padded, five-by-seven envelope addressed to her personally, not the PR department. But no return address.

Hmm.

She picked up the letter opener, slit the package and dumped the contents onto her desktop.

Out fell a royal-blue velvet pouch and a note printed in block script on high-quality paper.

You like to play games? Remember button, button, who's got the button? This is a new version called White Star, White Star, who's got the White Star? Is it you? Game on.

A shiver gripped her. What the hell was this? Could the White Star actually be in that bag?

With nervous fingers she dropped the note, yanked open the gathered tie of the pouch and dumped the contents into her palm.

But the White Star wasn't there.

Rather, it was an odd assortment of expensive jewelry. A four-carat diamond engagement ring. Sapphire earrings. An onyx brooch. A ruby ankle bracelet. Pearl necklace.

She picked up the pearls and rubbed them against her teeth. Natural, not cultured.

What was this all about?

She picked up the note and read it all the way through again, but it made no more sense the second

time than it had the first. Where had these jewels come
from? And who'd sent them to her?

Checking the envelope's postmark, she discovered
it had been mailed in Manhattan at 8:30 a.m. on the day
she'd bumped into Sam at Precinct 39.

"Wow," said waifish Mystique, who'd drifted in
through the open door. "Whose stones?"

"That's what I'd like to know."

Mystique picked up a diamond-and-sapphire necklace. "This looks like the one Zoey Zander used to wear."

"You knew Zoey Zander?"

"Sure. She used to come to all the fashion shows.
Had a thing for models."

"Oh, I didn't know."

"Too bad she's dead," Mystique said.

"Yeah, too bad."

The minute Mystique wandered out of the office,
Cass picked up the jewelry and held each piece to the
light. They winked and sparkled and shone brightly.

Was she actually looking at jewels stolen from the
Stanhope auction house?

She knew only one way to find out for sure.

Call Sam.

THE MINUTE SAM ENTERED the Isaac Vincent building,
he tensed. Partially in memory of his last momentous
visit here, but mostly over the fact that he was about to
come face to face with Cass again after giving her the
brush-off two days earlier.

He wasn't prepared.

You're here for the job. He told himself. *Just do your job.*

It sounded so damned reasonable in theory.

But in reality the minute Sam laid eyes on her, his heart started beating in a crazy, hapless rhythm.

The door to her office stood open. Cass was seated behind her desk, her hair anchored on top of her head with a pencil. She turned and leaned over to pull out the drawer of the file cabinet behind her.

Light from the window—that infamous window he'd crawled out of to rescue her off the ledge—fell across her cheek, casting her face in soft shadows. Today she was wearing her Hermès scarf as a belt, accentuating her narrow waist. The nape of her neck was exposed and the shoulder of her powder blue dress had slipped down just enough for him to see the strap of a powder-blue bra. But even in spite of that irregular display of lingerie, she looked regal, studious and perfectly contained, as if no one or nothing could touch her inner tranquility.

He caught his breath, stunned by her beauty. Bewildered by the way she made him feel inside.

When he'd first met her he'd thought her shallow and spoiled and far too sophisticated for a guy like him. He'd grossly underestimated her. She was as sharp as they came and beneath that sophisticated exterior lurked a girl-next-door wholesomeness that had gotten lost under the expensive shoes and fancy scarves and the crush of socialite parties.

Question was how lost had she become? In order to

support her lavish lifestyle had she turned to thievery? Had her values become that twisted? He didn't want to believe it, but he was a cop.

And she was his prime suspect.

He gulped and lightly rapped his knuckles against her door. "Knock, knock," he said.

Cass raised her head and the wary expression on her face sent an arrow through his heart.

"Sam." Her voice was cool as spring water. "Please, come in."

He crossed the threshold and closed the door behind him, wishing he could scoop her into his arms and kiss her. All the while knowing it would solve nothing.

The emotion, the tension, their undeniable chemistry electrified the air. He could see the finest tremor of her upraised chin. His own jaw was clenched so it wouldn't quiver and give him away.

His shoes trod heavily against the floor. His breath was reedy. Her gaze was fixed on his and he noticed her pupils widened as he neared.

Was it from guilt?

Or attraction?

When he reached her desk, he saw the royal blue velvet pouch sitting in the center. His eyes went to the bag, then back to her face.

"These the jewels?"

She nodded.

He pulled a pair of white latex gloves from his pocket, put them on and then gingerly picked up the pouch. He took out the jewels one by one and studied them closely.

"These are the pieces taken from the Stanhope robbery." He nodded. "Except for the White Star amulet. This was all you found in the package?"

"Yes."

"Where is the packaging it came in?"

She handed him the padded envelope. Her expression never changed, but her gaze kept going to his face, searching for some sign of emotion, some giveaway as to what he was feeling.

He could see the longing in her eyes and his heart slashed in two. He wanted to tell her that he cared about her. That the past weekend they'd shared together had meant a lot to him. That he wished things were different.

But they weren't different and he could not say those things. He could not make promises he could not keep. Sam studied the envelope as if his life depended on it and when he'd finished with it, he slipped the package in an evidence bag along with the jewels.

"Let me see the note."

She handed him the piece of notepaper and their fingers brushed slightly. Even through his latex glove, even that brief, fleeting touch, undid him. He inhaled. He had to keep himself closed off, show no emotion. If she had any inkling into how he really felt about her, he was screwed.

"'You like to play games?'" he read. "What do you suppose he means by that?"

"Or she," Cass said. "The letter writer could be a woman."

He knew that all too well. "Block print, dark lines

suggests a masculine hand, but we'll have a handwriting expert go over it."

"Why would the thief send me the jewels? It makes no sense."

Unless, in your remorse, you sent them to yourself.

"Maybe the thief is an admirer."

"Possibly."

They watched each other warily, playing a dangerous game of their own. Both dancing around what was really on their minds, what they really wanted to say but could not.

"But he or she, whatever the case may be, still has the White Star."

"Or so we're to assume."

"Okay, let's look at this rationally," Sam said, deciding that he was going to pretend for the moment that he was one hundred percent certain Cass was not involved in either the Stanhope robbery or the Blueblood Burglaries.

"I'm listening." She leaned back in her chair.

Sam paced. "He sends you jewelry that's worth somewhere in the neighborhood of two hundred thousand dollars. That's not chump change."

"Agreed." Her eyes stayed on him as he walked back and forth, back and forth across her small space.

"From what we can glean from the description of the White Star found in the auction house catalog, the amulet itself has no intrinsic value. The ivory, gold and carnelian that make up the White Star have a market value of about a hundred dollars. But the book you brought me indicates there's more to the amulet than meets the eye. I'm sending the book out to be translated, but I have a suspicion that to the right collector, the White Star would be priceless."

"Maybe," Cass said, "the White Star was the real target all along. Maybe the other items were just taken to throw the NYPD off the scent."

"Could be." He arched an eyebrow. He was toeing a tightrope here, not knowing how much to tell her, how much to hold back. He took a deep breath and asked the question that begged to be asked. "Thing is, Cass, why did the thief send Zoey Zander's jewelry to you?"

"You got me." She looked so completely guileless. How he wanted to believe that it was not an act.

"'White Star, White Star, who's got the White Star? Is it you?'" he read. "'Game on.'"

"That makes it sound as if he believes I have the White Star and maybe he's wanting to exchange the other jewelry for the amulet."

"Then why not just say that? Why the riddle?"

"I don't know."

Something nagged at Sam. He was missing something here. Something important. But he couldn't think what it was. Not with Cass sitting there, watching him, breathing so sweetly, her chest rising and falling to the rhythm that matched his fevered heartbeat.

His gaze fell to her lips.

She caught the shift and smiled, just barely but enough for him to know their private game was up. He had to get out of here. Now. Before he threw caution to the wind, destroyed all the evidence and begged her to run away with him to some distant tropical isle.

CASS HAD BEEN MISERABLE all day and it wasn't just from the hangover.

She couldn't stop thinking about the cold, methodical way Sam had come into her office, taken her statement, confiscated the jewels, grilled her as if she'd stolen the White Star and then turned around and walked back out again as if nothing had ever happened between them.

Any lingering hopes she'd been clinging to that he would change his mind about pursuing a relationship with her vanished.

He was finished. The unforgiving look in his eyes spoke the truth.

He wasn't interested.

Fine. Okay. She got it.

So why couldn't she let go?

It wasn't like her to cling. She prided herself on her spontaneous, fun-loving nature and her live-for-today outlook.

And as she stood in the subway, waiting for her stop, a stunning realization hit her. All her life she'd taken the hit-and-run approach to relationships. Perhaps that was even why she had such a fixation on shoes.

Shoes represented walking and walking meant freedom and freedom meant escape. She stayed in motion in order to suppress her guilt and regret over her actions.

She thought of all the men she'd dated. The men she'd wounded. She'd never meant to hurt any of them. She'd never even really been aware that she was causing them pain. She'd just been going merrily about her life, never recognizing that she'd actually been motivated by fear and anxiety.

Hiding beneath the cover of the next good time. While all along she'd been blindly, impulsively pursuing fun, without once considering the cost of her impulses.

Now Sam had turned the tables on her.

And it really hurt on the other side.

For the first time ever her "eat, drink and be merry" philosophy felt more like "play now pay later." She'd had her fun, the piper wanted his due.

She got off at her subway stop and trudged up Canal Street. Sadly, she thought of her Manolo Blahniks lost somewhere in the Catskills. First her shoes, now her man. It was turning out to be a crappy week for holding on to things. She should have checked her horoscope.

"Evenin' Cass," said the cheerful woman who mopped the floors in her building.

Cass forced a smile. "How are you, Sue?"

The older woman's eyes twinkled. Sue was a single mom, who took community college classes in the morning and cleaned in the evenings to make ends meet. "Good, very good actually. I finished my last computer class and I've got a job interview next Monday."

"That's wonderful news." Cass brightened.

"I can't thank you enough for encouraging me to go

back to school." Sue looked directly at her. "Your support has meant a lot to me and while it's been tough at
times, the effort has been worth it."

Cass blushed, embarrassed. "It was all you, Sue. I
don't deserve any credit."

"There were days when your belief in me was the
only thing keeping me in school. And thanks for telling
me about Suited for You. I would never have been able
to afford nice interview clothes on my own."

"You're welcome. I'm glad they could help."

Sue leaned on her mop and peered at her. "Are you
okay? You don't seem your usual self."

"Rough day at work," she mumbled.

"I'm sorry to hear that. Anything I can do to cheer
you up?"

"Just hearing about your job interview has already
lifted my spirits. I know you're going to ace it."

"That's so kind of you."

She gave Sue a quick hug, and then trudged upstairs
to her apartment, trying her best to think happy thoughts
but failing miserably. While she was happy for Sue, she
couldn't forget what she'd almost had with Sam.

Key in the lock. Almost inside her sanctuary. Home.
Where she could collapse on her bed and let herself cry
if that's what she wanted.

Except when she pushed open the door, she found
chaos instead of comfort.

Cass gasped and looked around.

Her cozy little home had been trashed. Kitchen
chairs overturned. Glass broken in the sink. Refriger-

ator left hanging open, condiments spilling out onto the laminate flooring.

Wearily, she kicked the door closed with her foot, dropped her purse and sank to the ground.

Well, hell. This just iced it.

SAM SAT ON A STOOL in the evidence lab. His shift was finished but he couldn't let go. The only fingerprints the lab tech had found on either the jewels or the inside of the envelope belonged to Cass. She couldn't have looked guiltier if she were walking around with a giant red downward-pointing arrow above her head.

Therein lay the problem.

It was all too handy. Too tidy. Too neatly tied up.

If Cass had stolen the jewels, then why send them to herself? And then call him to report it?

It made no sense.

And the main thing he couldn't reconcile was how she was able to rob Stanhope's. The auction house boasted state-of-the-art surveillance equipment and his research into Cass's background told him she possessed no skills in circumventing complex security systems.

He could buy her as the Blueblood Burglar. She's at a party, goes up to use the ladies' room, detours by the hostess's bedroom, steals a necklace or a toe ring or ankle bracelet from the jewelry box on the dresser. No one's the wiser until the party's over.

Sam had never believed that the two cases were related, but now his leading suspect in the Blueblood

Burglaries had received jewels from the Stanhope caper. Mailed to her from an anonymous source. Much too coincidental.

Unless someone was trying to frame her.

But who?

And why?

He kneaded his temples with his fingers. He was so tired, he couldn't think straight but he wasn't willing to give up. No matter how hard he tried, he couldn't shake the overwhelming feeling that he was missing something significant.

One by one, he picked up the pieces with his gloved hands, examining each under the light again and then matching them to the descriptive list of jewels stolen from the Zander collection. Every item was here and accounted for except for the White Star.

Why was it not with the rest of the gems? Where was the White Star? And maybe, most importantly, what was the amulet worth to the right person?

Sam held the antique onyx brooch under the high-powered lamp and for the first time noticed something dark on the sharp end of the stick pin.

Frowning, he narrowed his eyes.

Was that blood?

Excitement surged through him. By damn, it sure as hell looked like blood.

Don't get too fired up, he cautioned himself. The brooch was old. The blood could belong to Zoey Zander.

Still, it was the first good lead that didn't automatically point to Cass as the culprit.

"Hey, Joey," he called to the lab tech. "Have you tested for trace evidence on these items from the Stanhope robbery yet?"

"No, I've been swamped, but they're next on my list. So far, they've only been dusted for prints."

"Could you look at this a minute?"

The technician pried himself from the project he was working on and ambled over. "Find something?"

"This look like blood to you?"

Joey bent over to peer at the broach under the high-powered lighted magnifying glass. "Affirmative."

"Think it's enough for a DNA sample?"

Joey smiled. "Does the Pope…"

"Wear a funny hat? Yes, he does. Can you put a rush on it?"

Joey looked back at the project he'd just abandoned. "Working on a double homicide, here Sam. You're gonna have to wait."

"Do what you can, will ya? I need it sooner rather than later."

"I'll do my best."

"Thanks." Sam stood up and reached for his jacket. Finding the blood on the brooch had given him a second wind.

"Hey, bloodhound." One of the rookies stuck his head into the lab.

"Yeah?"

"Your uptown hottie just called. She says someone broke in to her apartment."

"What?"

The rookie repeated himself, but it had been a rhetorical question.

Sam was already out the door.

13

It took Sam nearly half an hour to get to Cass's place. Traffic jammed the streets and he finally abandoned the patrol car he'd jumped in outside the precinct. He jogged the last few blocks, praying she was all right, that she hadn't surprised the thief in the process of robbing her apartment.

A hundred thousand horrible images flashed into his mind. He tried to erase them, tried to tell himself everything was okay. But he was a cop and he knew too much to convince himself she was okay until he saw with his own eyes that she was unharmed.

He flashed his badge to the doorman, took the stairs two at a time to get to her apartment. Panting hard, he banged on her door. "Cass, it's me, Sam. Open up."

She pulled open the door, peeked nervously out at him. "I didn't know they were going to send you. I figured you'd already left for the day."

He was so glad to see her, to find out that she was all right, that it was all Sam could do not to cover her face in kisses in a total meltdown.

Her hair was pulled back in a ponytail and her face

was scrubbed free of cosmetics. She wore sweatpants, an old Yankees T-shirt—which made him smile in memory of their Mets versus Yankees conversation in the Catskills—worn thin from so many washings and a pair of dark green slouch socks. In one hand she held a broom and dustpan.

The girl next door.

This whole other side of her, unexpected and delightful, escalated his emotional turmoil. The cop arm-wrestling with the man. A rational mind brawling with a lover's heart.

"The Cinderella chic is working for you." He struggled to sound light and hide his inner conflict. "May I come in?"

"Sorry to look like such a mess." She glanced down at her attire. "After having my space violated I just had to take a long hot shower and slip into my favorite lazy clothes so I could feel more like me."

More like me. The words were resonant with meaning. Was Princess Glam, at heart, really just an ordinary woman?

"I like it," he said gruffly.

"Come on in." She stood aside, didn't look at him directly, as if she was afraid to make eye contact.

I'm afraid too, he wanted to say, but he couldn't find a way to say it.

Sam looked around. The place had been tossed, but not by professionals. It looked more like someone venting their rage. His nose twitched. Underneath the pungent cleaner she was using he caught the scent of a damp, earthy, woodsy smell that seemed familiar but he couldn't identify amid the stronger chemicals.

"You shouldn't have started cleaning up," he said, the cop in him winning out for the moment.

"Oh." She blinked. "I didn't think about disturbing the evidence. Honestly, I wasn't sure the NYPD would even be interested in my little break-in."

"Anything missing?"

"I don't think so. I looked all through my things and I couldn't find anything missing. A lot of stuff is smashed up, though. I checked my roommate Elle's room and whoever did this didn't touch her stuff, so apparently it was personal." She was talking excessively. Sam understood why.

"You're certain nothing is missing?"

"Pretty sure, but I'll double check."

He followed her to her tiny bedroom, stood in the doorway, watching while she went through the room again, opening drawers, searching closets. The intruder had strewn her clothes all around. A pair of scarlet thong panties hung from the mirror, a purple bra was draped over a lampshade. Her shoes had been dumped in a heap in the middle of the floor. Books pulled from shelves. Papers scattered.

Cass spotted something on the floor, paused and snatched it up. It was a school yearbook. A loose photograph fluttered out and landed at Sam's feet.

He bent to pick it up. It was a picture of Cass when she was fifteen or sixteen with another young girl. They were the same height, both thin and vibrant but where

Cass was blond, the other girl was a brunette. They had their arms slung around each other and were posing in front of a bright red Mustang convertible.

Sam flipped the picture over. On the back, in the loopy scrawl of a teenage girl were written the words: *Nikki and Cass, friends forever.*

"Nikki?"

"Old friend." Cass leapt across the room, snatched the photograph from his hand, stuffed it back between the pages of her yearbook. She kept her head down and she was breathing hard.

What in the hell was that all about?

Sam wouldn't push. The photograph wasn't related to the break-in. It was none of his business. She was entitled to her secrets.

They stood on opposite sides of her chaotic bedroom, her plump sleigh bed sandwiched between them. He studied her, intrigued.

It was the wrong time, the wrong place, the wrong everything, but her beauty was luring him in, pulling him down. He knew better, and yet he could not resist looking at her. With her Wedgwood-blue eyes, full pink lips and leggy figure, she fluoresced.

Cass plopped down on the edge of her bed and drew a pillow to her chest. "Everything is such a mess, I honestly can't say for certain whether anything is missing or not."

"I noticed the lock on your front door didn't appear to have been forced."

"No."

"Do you ever leave your windows open?"

"In the heat of the summer sometimes, but I haven't opened them this year."

Sam walked to the window, almost brushing her knees as he went past. She shrank back from touching him and that just made him feel bad. Was her reaction from the shock of having her apartment upended or was it more personal? Was she that disturbed by the thought of their legs coming into contact?

Shaking off his thoughts, he peered out the window at the fire escape below and started to get queasy just looking down four floors. The window was latched from the inside. If the intruder had come in through here, he had locked the window behind him and left through the front door.

Unless Cass had locked the window.

Unless she'd ransacked her own place and made the whole thing up.

Sam shifted uncomfortably, not wanting to believe that. "Does anyone have a key to your place?"

Her face was mobile in its responsiveness, her smooth forehead corrugating in a frown when she was deep in thought, her lips tightening, her head bobbing up and down to register her agreement. "My parents, my sister, Morgan, and my roommate, Elle."

"Could your roommate have come back from her tour early?"

Cass shook her head. "I just spoke to Elle last night. She's in Vancouver."

"Did she give out a key to anyone?"

"I don't know. But her room wasn't plundered. Just mine and the rest of the apartment."

"How about your sister? Do you two get along?"

"Morgan would never trash my place. She's six years older and always acted like a second mother. Besides, she lives in Connecticut. I can't see her popping up here on the train, trashing my apartment and zipping off again."

"Anybody you know could have gotten hold of your key? Family, friends, acquaintances? Who's been in your place recently?"

"Basically you're saying I should suspect everyone."

"Yeah."

Unless of course this was all staged for your benefit, his cop voice pointed out.

"That's what your life is like, isn't it? The way your mind thinks. You always have to assume the worst about people."

Sam grimaced. She was right. He did have to assume the worst about everyone. Including her.

"Oh, this just sucks." Her shoulders trembled and Sam feared she was going to start crying. She looked so vulnerable, so incredibly fragile that he couldn't resist comforting her. Plunking down beside her on the bed, he drew her gently into the crook of his arm.

She leaned her head against his shoulder and dammit, he was lost. Sam didn't care where the evidence pointed. She could not be a thief. He felt it in his gut, in his heart, in his soul. She was not playing. Her emotions were real. He could feel every one of them in each shuddering breath she took.

"It's okay." He patted her head. "You've been through a lot. You can cry if you want to."

And cry she did, burying her face against him and sobbing her heart out.

Her despair twisted him all up inside. He was used to seeing her upbeat, flirtatious.

"Come on, sweetheart. It's all right."

"I've had a very crappy week," she said.

"It's only Wednesday."

"Still."

"I thought the weekend was pretty damned great. Well, except for the falling out of the tree part."

She pulled away. "That's not how you acted when I came to see you."

"I'm sorry about that."

"Why did you break things off with me?"

He told her part of the truth if not all of it. "You're out of my league, Cass Richards. I knew I couldn't keep a woman like you interested for long. I guess I figured break it off with you before you could break it off with me."

"Oh, Sam." She reached up to stroke his cheek with her fingertip.

"Be honest, Cass. You've admitted you're not into commitment and I like you too much to get in any deeper, knowing that our affair could never lead to anything serious."

"Never say never," she murmured. "Or that's what my mother keeps telling me."

"I didn't mean to hurt you," he vowed. "Please forgive me if I did. It was self-preservation."

She canted her head. "You're not like most cops."

"No?"

"You're not cynical or hard-boiled."

"What am I?"

"Pragmatic."

"That's not very flattering."

"It's a compliment. I wish that I could be more sensible. Maybe I wouldn't end up on window ledges or climbing trees for amulets. I have this terrible habit of looking before I leap."

"Except when it comes to intimacy," Sam said.

"Yeah," she agreed. "Except for that."

"Intimacy and I aren't on the best of speaking terms either, if that makes you feel any better," he said. "It's hard, laying yourself open to another person, really trusting them completely."

"How *hard* is it?" She giggled.

"There you go, making fun."

"You're right," she admitted. "I do tend to turn the conversation light when things get too serious. Bad habit."

"There's a cure."

"Really?"

"Yeah," he said tentatively, wondering how she would respond to his suggestion, nervous about how this was going to play out. "We could each tell the other something intimate about ourselves, something we rarely talk about. Or we could confess something that's been bothering us, something we've wanted to tell each other but haven't been able to find a way to do it."

"Anything I tell you will be kept in confidence? I mean I can trust you, can't I?"

They looked at each other, neither saying anything, the tension building. He was taking a gamble here, both professionally and emotionally. He had no idea what she was going to tell him. What she might confess and how it would affect their relationship.

"You can trust me," he said. "Tell you what, I'll go first."

She waited.

"Remember when I told you that I was married once?"

"Uh-huh. You said she left you because you weren't rich enough for her."

"Well," he said. "That was only part of it."

"What didn't you tell me?"

"I'd come home from work and find Keeley with new things. Jewelry, shoes, scarves. I'd yell at her for blowing our money on frivolous things when we were supposed to be saving to buy a house. She told me she'd bought the stuff at sales and discount stores. Because I wanted to make the marriage work I decided to believe her."

Cass shifted beside him, her eyes on his face.

"Every day it was something new. A purse, a skirt, a diamond necklace. My sister Beth told me the items were not the sort of things you'd pick up at sales or discount stores. Finally, I confronted Keeley and learned she'd been getting credit cards behind my back and when she maxed them all out, she'd borrow from people, including an ex-boyfriend."

Sam bit down on his bottom lip. He'd never learned exactly how Keeley had paid back her old boyfriend. He hadn't been able to face that particular truth. She'd killed any love he'd once had for her and the fact that she'd turned to another man in order to feed her shopping habit had wounded his male ego.

"Sam." Cass placed a hand on his arm. "I'm so sorry, that must have been awful for you."

She made a soft, plaintive sound of sympathy that cut him to the quick. Now he couldn't stop talking. He needed more of her trust, needed more of the understanding expression in her eyes. Odd yearning for a man who buried his feelings. Perhaps this urge to talk excessively was punishment for the mistakes he'd made. The decisions he regretted. Sam felt both relieved and condemned.

"The harder I worked the more Keeley bought. She swore she'd stopped but I'd find a new dress hidden among the clothes. Or unearth a new pair of sandals buried under the garbage bags in the broom closet. I realized she had a problem and couldn't stop. She had an emptiness inside I didn't fill. She started writing hot checks on a bank account she'd opened under a false name using a stolen ID."

"What did you do?"

"I arrested her for fraud. I'm a cop. What else could I do?"

"That must have been so hard for you."

"She started divorce proceedings the minute her lawyer got her out of jail."

"That's so sad."

"It was for the best. So that's my big secret. Go ahead, let loose, ask me anything and I'll tell you the truth." He held her gaze.

She thought for a moment, nibbling her bottom lip in a way that made him want to kiss her so badly that his own lips tingled. "How come you became a cop in the first place? Does it run in your family like most cops? Was your dad in law enforcement?"

"Good question. No one in my family is a cop." He paused a moment, moistening his lips before continuing. Cass had gone straight to the hardest question she could have asked. "When I was ten and my kid sister Janie was seven my mom sent us to the corner store for milk. My mom told me to hold Janie's hand, but some kids on our block saw us walking together and they started poking fun at me."

Cass laid her palm over his chest and looked up into his eyes. "Your heart's beating faster."

"Yeah, well, telling this gets to me worse than the Keeley story."

"You don't have to go through with it, if it's too painful."

"No," he said. "That's our deal. If we're going to trust each other we have to get our secrets out in the open."

Initially, when he'd began this, his point had been to get her to spill her secrets but now he found he wanted her to know the events that shaped him.

"So I'm walking way ahead of Janie. She's calling out to me, begging me to wait up, but I ignore her. I head into the crosswalk and I'm almost on the other side of the street when this car comes speeding around the corner."

"Sam," Cass whispered. "Your sister, no."

He nodded, the old guilt rising up inside him. "Yeah."

"Was she…?"

"Hit and run. The impact broke her back." He pinched the bridge of his nose, struggling to hold back the emotions. Hell, he wasn't going to cry in front of Cass. Not over something that happened twenty-three years ago.

"How horrible for your family."

"It was bad for a long time. But Janie pulled through and had no lasting brain damage. She'll always be in a wheelchair but she's married a great guy and they adopted a baby."

"That's amazing about your sister. What happened to the driver?"

"The police were determined. They didn't stop looking for the guy until they caught him. He was drunk, driving with a suspended license. My parents were so relieved once the police took him off the streets and I knew right then and there that I wanted to be a cop. That I wanted to bring hope into the lives of grieving families. To stop the criminals who hurt people."

"What did your folks think about your career decision?"

"My parents had their reservations when I chose

law enforcement, but it's who I am and they accepted it. And it turns out I like being a cop. I like doing work that matters in people's lives."

She said nothing after he'd finished his story, just leaned over and gently pressed her lips against his.

He gathered her to his chest.

Their kiss was like that of old lovers meeting after a long separation, a tentative approach, a shock of recognition and then the happy realization they still belonged together.

She reached for the buttons on his shirt and he let her undo them one by one, her slowness deliberate but not teasing. Once his shirt was pushed open, baring his chest, her nimble fingers crawled along the surface of his skin, mapping out each muscle, feeling the texture, learning the language of his body.

Her tiny bedroom with its pale purple walls was their cocoon. They stripped off her chenille bedspread, pulling down the blankets and the top sheet. Kicked off their clothes, tossed them onto the muddled heap on the floor.

Sam held her close and kissed her, sweetly, leisurely. Breathed in the scent of her, drew her into his body, held her down deep in his lungs, coddling her gently and turned her scent loose again with his exhalation and realized that he was forever altered.

Life had taught him to be guarded. Janie's accident, his bad first marriage, his job as a cop. All bricks in the mortar of his stony castle and letting down the drawbridge of his defenses, spanning the moat of his self-protection, letting Cass inside the fortress of his soul, left him vulnerable and weak-kneed.

Sam extended his trembling hand.

She locked eyes with him and accepted his embrace. She melted against his chest, melted into his heart.

Their tongues met. Where they touched, they were no longer two but one. Skin against skin. Muscle against muscle. Breath against breath.

They fell into the mattress, in a knot of need and impassioned limbs. Sam claimed one of her nipples, suckling it gently until she writhed beneath him, begging for more.

She fondled him in places that drove him to the brink and he repaid her in kind until they were both hovering, both humming, both hungering for release.

When they could stand it no more, he thrust himself into her. She opened up the intimate workings of her body to him, adding his organ to hers as if it was meant to be there all along.

This was the ultimate risk.

And he was falling in love with her.

No. That wasn't right. He'd already fallen. Fallen so far and so hard that he knew he would never ever be the same again.

The understanding had been there for days, but he'd told himself it was only sex. He'd refused to examine the veracity of what had been happening and now, it was too late. But honestly, could he have stopped the plunge, even if he'd heeded the warning signs?

He felt as if he'd entered an exalted land after a long

and arduous journey. She'd touched a primal nerve inside him. Her ability to fly with her body, to soar airborne in his arms.

Her indomitable life force drew him. A magnet of desire. Her tempestuous, headlong spirit embraced him like wind and weather, desert and danger.

There, somewhere in the mysterious swirl of their joining, he found paradise.

Afterward, as they lay sated in each other's arms, he leisurely stroked his fingers over her breast.

"Tell me," he whispered. "Tell me something special about yourself. Something no one else in the world knows."

14

CASS HESITATED. Emotional intimacy took high-wire courage. Was she ready? What if she got swallowed up by him? Suffocated? Dismantled? What if she forgot who she was?

But he'd gone out on a limb for her. Telling her about his sister, her accident, how he'd felt responsible. How he had become a cop as a way to make amends for traveling too far ahead of Janie in the crosswalk.

About how he'd been unable to fulfill his ex-wife's needs. About how he'd had to arrest her for fraud. That had to have been a difficult choice.

He'd talked and talked, and if she wanted to keep him, she knew she must talk, too.

Slowly, bit by bit, she told him the story of the school carnival and how winning the cake walk had turned into a terrifying experience.

And when she was done he didn't laugh, didn't act as if her story was unimportant. By some miracle, he seemed to know how much she'd put on the line.

He kissed her and touched his forehead to hers and looked deep into her eyes, into the very center of her.

"Now," he said, "tell me why it's really so hard for you to make a choice and stick with it."

Cass sucked in her breath. "I...I can't."

He leaned over her, his posture suddenly imposing. His lips pressed into a firm line, his eyes demanding. "I shared my secrets with you."

She squirmed. "I told you about the cakes."

"Not emotional enough." He tapped her chin. "I want to know the real you. I want to know why your shoes and your scarf are so important to you."

"They're not important to me." She shrugged.

"Did you know that your face turns blotchy when you lie?"

Cass reached up and touched her flaming hot cheeks. Damn. He'd caught her.

"If it's no big deal, then why not tell me how you feel?" he asked.

"Because it's private."

"That's what this is about, Cass, you and me sharing private stuff, getting to know each other as intimately as possible."

"I'm not sure I can," she confessed.

Sam looked disappointed and she felt as if she'd reneged on a serious vow.

"It's okay," he said. "I understand. I couldn't talk about Janie's accident for years afterward, but it wasn't until I did start talking about it that I came to terms with the fact that she would never walk again. Once I accepted it, that's when my life fully began. Before that I was just running away."

"I'm not running away."

He didn't contradict her. He just watched in that somber, assessing way of his.

"Having nice things makes me feel good about myself and if I feel good, then everything will turn out all right. Having to make choices, having to pick one path over another makes me anxious that I'll miss out on something glorious waiting just around the corner."

Sam nodded, acting as if what she'd said made perfect sense. But how could he understand her when she didn't understand her own impulses?

"I'm listening. There's something more you're not telling me."

Cass swallowed. She and Sam did have tragedy in common but she wasn't sure it was the kind of thing you should bond over.

"Remember the picture you saw that fell out of my yearbook?"

"Nikki and Cass, friends forever?"

"Yeah."

"I'm guessing it wasn't forever."

She shook her head. "Nikki was my best friend in high school. We were like sisters. We were always over at each other's houses. We never fought. Not even over guys."

Sam propped his head on his hand, palm against his ear, his gray eyes intent as he listened.

"Then Nikki got sick during our senior year. Leukemia."

Cass choked back the tears burning her throat and closed her eyes. This was much harder than she'd thought it would be and she's thought it would be pretty damned hard. The old feelings of shame and regret came rushing back.

"It's all right," he said. "I get the picture. You don't have to say anything more."

"No," she said. "You're right. I just buried my feelings down deep inside and pretended it didn't hurt as badly as it did. I'm just warning you, I'm probably going to cry."

He opened his arms. "I've got big shoulders."

She rolled into his embrace, pressing her face against his chest. He held her tightly. After a moment, she felt strong enough to continue.

"I tried to be a good friend to Nikki. I tried to stick by her. I went to her treatments with her and told jokes to make her laugh. When her hair fell out, I bought her a nice scarf to wear."

She paused, staring into the past. "I tried, but it was too difficult. Gradually, I went to see her less and less. I just couldn't stand watching her suffer." She brought a hand to her mouth. "I couldn't deal with it. I was a coward."

"Cut yourself some slack. You were only a kid."

"In the end I stopped going to visit her. Period. I went off to college and when I came home I didn't even drop by her house. A couple of months later my parents called to tell me that she'd passed away. I didn't even go to the funeral."

"I bet Nikki understood."

"I didn't even understand my behavior. How could

she? It was then I realized I wasn't the kind of person who could handle the grim realities of life. I was better off flitting from friend to friend, from guy to guy than getting too involved. That way I'd never let anyone down again."

"It's time to stop beating yourself up over what happened. Be kind to you." Tenderly he traced his fingertips over her heart.

At that endearing gesture, something inside Cass broke loose. Something she'd been holding on to for far too long. Guilt for being the healthy one, anger at herself for not being able to hang in there with Nikki's illness, sorrow for what she'd lost.

She was swamped in emotions. She shuddered, sobbing against Sam's shoulder.

"Shh, sweetheart. What about your parents, your sister, your coworkers, your other friends? You haven't let them down." He tucked her tighter into the crook of his arm. "Don't you realize what a truly amazing person you are? You're so vibrant and alive. So much fun to be around. Everyone lights up when you walk into a room."

"Really?" She swiped at her face with the back of a hand.

"You didn't know that?"

She shook her head.

"Well, they do. You inspire people. You inspire me. You're an idealist, Cass. You see the very best in people and the world. That's a rare gift and I treasure it in you. Your excitement makes me excited. I'm more of me when I'm with you."

"Oh, Sam." She breathed and in reverence lifted her eyes to his face and let him into her heart. They lost themselves in looking at each other. He was safety and adventure, risk and faith and she wanted him more than she'd ever wanted any man.

The sound of his voice, deep and sensual, filled up her ears, massaged her body with low-level vibrations. Foreign enough to keep her adrenaline flowing, yet familiar enough that it also produced a light, floaty feeling as if she were suspended in clouds.

In her brain, the synapses were firing like mad transmitting messages, the ultimate broadband, signaling her cell membranes, telling her to open up. Open up all the way. Not just with her body, not just with her mind, but with all her heart.

This one is different.

The night in the laundry room with him had been fun, sexy and gratifying, but this…this was different. This was exceptional, the purest sexual encounter she'd ever had.

Skydiving, blind, fervent, playing with fire, magnificent. They were ferocious, famished, fond, fraught, feasting, feeding, frantic.

"Take me," she commanded, urgent and pleading. "Make me."

Her plea excited them both.

The little jolts in her brain pushed tingles down her spine, then out through her limbs and along the surface of her skin.

She fell back against the pillow, her gaze tracking his body. He was lean and taut-skinned, with a ladder of muscle that rippled from his abdomen to his chest. She could not stop thinking what those flexing muscles felt like beneath the planes of her palms, the down of her cheek, the inside of her thigh.

Cass felt turned inside out, the soft pink tender underside of her showing, exposed and yes, yes, yes, he knew it. Knew what she needed.

He slipped his fingers into her scorching center. She rode his palm, thinking of the ocean, how it ebbed and flowed. Such strong shimmering movements.

His fingers dripped with her juices, slick and sweet. Sam was straddled above her, on his knees, his thick hard erection jutting proud and ready again.

He moaned.

She sat up, pushed him back against the mattress. Took him in her mouth, licking, sucking, thinking, *I've never known any man like him. I could stay with this one. Forever and ever doesn't scare me. Not with him.*

"No," he said and gently reached down to touch her mouth, breaking their contact. "Not this way. I want to come inside you. This is special. You're special."

And Cass knew it was true.

He was so good at making her feel good. When they moved together it was like a dance, an attunement. His leg there, hers here. His back arched just so, then her own. Even when they turned and tumbled so that she surfaced straddling him it was graceful, adroit, as though they were suspended.

Had it been this way from the beginning, smooth as a globe, an act of beauty as well as an act of love?

Though the start had only been a few days ago, Cass found it difficult to remember her former self, who she'd been before him: impulsive but charming, self-centered she now knew.

But here she was with him feeling—what was it? Ah yes, accepted, supported, cared for.

They were both aware of every nuanced murmur of their bodies. They were swept away by the slightest touch, barely able to breath.

They switched again, him on top and unhurriedly, he pressed himself into her, thrusting steadily until he was buried to the hilt. A breaker of uncontainable desire rushed over her. She milled herself against his pelvic bone, grinding hard. Fisting her hands into the Egyptian cotton of her crisp four hundred thread count sheets.

"Sam, oh, Sam. That feels so good. That's right. Give it to me."

"You like that?"

"Yes."

"You want me?"

"Yes, yes."

He increased the tempo of his thrusts, moving in and out of her with a rhythmic precision that drove her mad. With each inward plunge, she felt abundant, almost to the point of explosion. It wasn't enough.

"Faster," she pleaded. "I need you faster."

His cadence quickened.

"More, more." Her voice sounded hoarse and needy, echoing off the walls.

He gave her everything she asked for.

Cass lost touch with the commonplace, let go of all fears, released her grip on the earth, upon reality. Deliriously, they were transcended, dazed and drunken.

And that's when Cass Richards realized for the first time in her life she'd fallen hopelessly, helplessly in love.

LATER SHE WOKE to find him beside her, his leg thrown over her waist, his hair sexily tousled, his gaze upon her face. Cass closed her eyes and smiled as he leaned in for a kiss.

Sam nuzzled her cheek lightly. She raised her eyelids halfway, still smiling and their eyes met in greeting. She teased him, playing coy.

His skin was damp with a fine outline of sweat between his shoulder blades. He looked at her in a way that made her feel like the sexiest woman alive. She thought she knew her body well, but in his eyes, she was changed, charting unexplored territories of her sexuality.

Sam closed her arms around his neck. She leaned her face into him, smelling his essence, resting her chin against his soft, dark brown chest hairs. They lay there unmoving, mesmerized by the sounds of their own breathing.

Cass slowly became aware of the pressure of their touching bodies. She pushed back from him, kissing his arms as they slid away from her neck.

Eyes flashing, he inched his fingertips up the inside of her thigh. A laugh, sweet and thick as honey, caught in her throat making her sound like one of those smoky-voiced French cabaret singers, husky and exotic. She was turning into someone new.

And he was her conduit. She was becoming her essential self. In the process, learning to let go of the belief that she needed Hermès scarves and filet mignon and limo rides in order to feel satisfied. She was naked and in her nakedness she was able to fully assimilate her experience and be nourished by it. She required nothing beyond this ecstacy.

She grasped his shoulders to steady the fluttering of her heart against the tingling pleasure of his touch. He lowered his head, rested it on the roundness of her belly. Her breath came quicker, deeper. A flush of awareness tickled the back of her throat.

He raised his head and looked at her. They looked frankly into each other's eyes. Not talking, just looking. Cass saw something that she'd never seen in a man's face after lovemaking. Was it honesty? A trueness only real and lasting intimacy brings?

What did her eyes tell him? Could he see that this experience was new to her? These feelings. This letting down of the guard. This willingness to leap with him into the arms of an unknown destiny.

Recognition passed between them. A vow unspoken.

His erection stirred against her thigh, growing hard and hot all over again. She reached down to slowly caress his shaft, admiring the throb.

Anticipation sparked in his eyes as she increased the measured stroking. He moaned when she cupped his balls with her other hand. She marveled at their weight,

felt them tighten up against his crotch, felt a corre-
sponding pressure, a tightening of her own nerves.

She bent her head. Kissed his satiny tip, tasted his
pungent tang. She dragged her tongue down one side
of him, tracing his pattern.

He groaned.

Her tongue traveled, roaming over the brilliant territory. As her excitement grew, her control slipped. Her
mouth closed delicately over the head of him.

Sam lay motionless, straining against his impulses.
She clutched his hips with both hands, sucked him first
slowly all the way to his tip, turning her head so she could
feel every part of him. Then down to the base of his shaft.

Cass dove, her tongue swirling, in one fluid movement.

Sitting up, she moved her hands around his buttocks
to the inside of his firm, muscular thighs. Gently she
stroked, moving over his thighs with shivering light-
ness. She glided with him as smoothly as breathing, inhaling him and then allowing him to fall away on a sigh.

Yet the whole time she was holding back, holding
something in reserve. Their pace quickened and they
never lost contact. They swayed in unison.

"Cass, Cass, Cass," he groaned, his head thrown
back, his eyes tightly closed.

His body went rigid. The signal she was looking for.
The signal to wait.

Cass did not move, her mouth resting on the base of
his shaft. The head of him pounding inside her.

He shuddered in premonition.

She wrapped her legs around his thighs so he could feel her warm wetness, dripping with excitement. She undulated her hips in rhythm with her mouth, moving up and down him once more.

His hands reached for her. He touched her hair. His fingers moved blindly over her shoulders, trying to find a place to hold on to as he arched his back.

She wriggled away from his hands, determined to focus all her attention on his pleasure, knowing he would return it tenfold. She closed her eyes, calmed her pulsing heart. All her awareness was in her fingers and her tongue.

He was close. So very close.

His breath came in rough gasps. Her body simmered in sweet sweat as they rocked together. She moved her mouth and her fingers took over. With a burst and shudder he came. His juices leaking over her hand onto his belly.

He cried her name.

And she collapsed against him. Together, they lay breathing heavily, absorbed by vibrant bliss.

SAM WOKE WITH THE NEED to do something special for Cass. He propped himself up on one elbow and lay watching her sleep, his heart a leap frog in his chest.

He'd been ruined. She'd wrecked him for any other woman.

And he was delirious about his downfall.

She was the sexiest thing in the world and he wanted her all the time. They had such fun together. Both in bed and out of it. He loved the way she was delighted by life. And her delight, delighted him. Her instincts were delicate, beautiful things, and it was painful, but wonderful to realize the way she handled him. It wasn't guile on her part. It was just the way she was and he was wrapped tightly around her pinkie.

After Keeley, he'd feared he might never be able to fully open up to a woman again, but his feelings for Cass overrode the past. His need for connection was stronger than his fear of being hurt.

He knew she needed more time, that her fear of commitment wouldn't disappear overnight, that she hadn't really known him long enough to be sure she could count on him. That was fine. He had all the patience in the world. In the meantime, he was going to set about showing her exactly how much she meant to him.

And that she could trust him to be there for her, no matter what.

Sam eased from the bed without waking her, collected his clothes off the floor and slipped out of her bedroom to get dressed. He finished cleaning up the mess the intruder had made of her kitchen knowing at this point it was more important to get her life back to normal than to gather evidence on a break-in where nothing had been stolen.

As he puttered, he found himself humming the Madonna song "Angel." Hell, he didn't even like Madonna, but the song just fit.

When he'd finished setting her kitchen to rights, he

moved to making breakfast. He opened the fridge to see what she had.

Bottled water. Olives. Two oranges. A dozen packets of soy sauce. Mustard. Three eggs. A tub of margarine and an half-gallon carton of two percent milk.

Sam smiled. Ah, the life of a hip, young, urban single.

He looked in the cupboard, found both a half loaf of bread and an unopened bottle of maple syrup. French toast it was.

Cracking open the fridge once more, he tucked the eggs under his arm and reached for the milk. Hmm. There was something lumpy in the bottom of the milk carton. Had it curdled?

He set the eggs on the counter and wrinkled his nose as he opened the carton, preparing for the smell of soured milk. But it wasn't curdled.

Whatever the something was in the bottom shifted heavily. Weird.

Sam took a tall glass from the cabinet, poured off the milk into it and then squeezed open the entire top of the carton and peered inside.

Jewelry.

Why did she have jewelry in her milk carton?

He carried the loot over to the sink and rinsed it off. As soon as he'd washed away the milky film from the gems, his stomach sickened.

They were all here.

Everything the Blueblood Burglar had stolen. The teardrop pendant that had gone missing during the Ackermans' party, the cameo from the Martindales'. A

Tiffany watch from the Parkers. And most telling of all, the chunk of jade from Bunnie Bernaldo's Buddha.

His world caved in. A landslide. An avalanche. Burying him alive.

He'd been so sure she was innocent. Convinced of it. Staked his future on it. His gut had deceived him. His heart had lied.

Accepting the truth wasn't easy. Desperately, he wracked his brain, searching for any other possible explanation for how the Blueblood Burglar booty had gotten into her milk carton.

And the reasons he concocted were beyond belief. No good cop would have accepted them. In the end, he was left with one conclusion.

His angel was an outlaw.

15

"WHAT'S THIS?" Sam loomed over her bed, his cupped hands extended in front of him.

Cass sat up blinking, not understanding what was going on. What was he talking about? Groggily, she pushed her hair from her face.

"What were these doing in your milk carton?"

She shook her head, still not comprehending. The dark expression on his face scared her. "What are you talking about?"

He shoved his palms under her nose and for the first time she saw the jewelry. Her mouth dropped open.

Around his thumb was looped the Tiffany watch that had gone missing the night of her friend Melina's birthday party. There winked the cluster diamond earrings stolen from her coworkers' Easter celebration. And in the center of his palm sat the round green jade from Bunnie's Buddha.

As she stared at the treasures in Sam's hands, understanding crept over her. Every piece of jewelry in his hand had been pilfered during elaborate parties thrown by luminaries and the social elite. All parties she had attended.

Every single one of them.

She looked up to meet Sam's gaze, clutching the sheet to her breast, acutely aware of her nakedness.

He said nothing, just clenched his jaw. His face changed. Went white. With anger or hurt she didn't know which. But he had no right to be hurt or angry. She was the injured party here. She was the one he was wrongly accusing of a crime with his murky gray eyes.

"You think I stole these?"

"They were in the milk carton in your refrigerator," he repeated.

"Well then, someone else is trying to frame me. My apartment was vandalized. Find out who broke in and you'll find out who's put them there."

"There's no sign of forced entry."

She couldn't have been more shocked if he'd kicked her in the gut with his thick, ugly Doc Martens boots. "You think I wrecked my own place?"

Cass had never seen such emotions in a man's face all at once. Regret, disappointment, grimness, steely resolve.

"I don't want to think it, Cass. Show me something else. Give me something I can cling to."

Another unpleasant thought slapped her.

"You didn't take me to Bunnie's for an introduction because you suspected she and Trevor had robbed the Stanhope auction house. You were spying on me, waiting to see if I would steal something."

His guilty expression was answer enough. He shifted his weight, his hands still outstretched, the jewelry winking at her in accusation.

"Yeah."

A short, derisive noise escaped her. Unbelievable. She'd finally, *finally* fallen for a man and look where it had gotten her. "You thought I was guilty from the very beginning. You've been using me all along, trying to get me to crack. Lovely technique, Detective Mason."

"No." He shook his head. "Last night was…"

"A bad mistake," she said firmly. Cass tightened her jaw. She wasn't going to cry. She refused to cry. She was tougher than that. She was innocent. She'd get a lawyer. She'd prove she hadn't stolen anything.

And her feelings for Sam?

Well, clearly that was over.

"You have the right to remain silent," he said.

SAM SAT WITH HIS BACK to the wall at O'Reilly's bar two blocks from the 39th Precinct, planning on getting rip-roaring drunk. Putting Cass in jail had been the single most difficult thing he'd ever done in his life. And he hated himself for it.

But what choice had he had?

His gut told him she was innocent, but the evidence said otherwise. He was a cop, sworn to uphold the law.

He'd done the dutiful thing.

But was doing his duty the right thing?

Gritting his teeth, Sam knocked back a swig of beer. He hated to believe he had a pattern of falling for shallow beautiful women.

No. He refused to accept that. Yes, on the surface,

Cass and Keeley were a lot alike. But underneath, they were midnight and dawn. Cass had a generous heart. She was kind and considerate of others. She was fun loving yes, and that was part of the reason he was so attracted to her. She balanced out his more serious side.

Unless he was simply deceiving himself.

Was he?

Sam plowed a hand through his hair. He knew Cass must be feeling powerfully betrayed. Last night, he'd made her promises. Promises he'd been unable to keep. He couldn't blame her if she hated his guts.

Right now, he hated his own guts.

Sam's cell phone vibrated against his hip. He didn't want to answer it. Wanted nothing more than to get stinking drunk and forget all about Cass Richards.

But the phone wouldn't stop buzzing. Finally, he snatched it up. "Yeah?"

"Sam? This is Joey from the evidence lab. Got that DNA report back from that blood sample you found on the onyx brooch recovered from the Stanhope robbery."

Sam sat up straighter, his heart a piston in his chest. "What did you find?"

"There were two donors on the specimen."

"Two?"

"But neither one of them matched your suspect, Cass Richards."

His sigh of relief was audible. "Did you find a match?"

"One was unidentifiable. We did get a hit on the second, but I don't think it's going to help you much," Joey said.

"What do you mean?"

"It was a match to the contractor the Stanhope hired to assess and catalogue the Zander estate. It's highly likely the guy stuck himself while he was logging in the items, probably has nothing to do with your case."

"You gonna give me a name, Joey?" Sam spat out the question.

"Sure, sure. It's Marcos Rebisi."

Sam hung up the phone, bolted from the bar. He knew now what the smell was he'd detected underneath the antiseptic scent in Cass's apartment. It was the same odor he'd smelled in the stairwell of the rehab hospital.

Wet cardboard.

The damp boxy smell of Marcos Rebisi's cologne.

He had to get to Cass. Had to find out exactly what had happened between her and Marcos.

Sam couldn't believe he'd been so shortsighted. He'd gone through the roster of Stanhope employees, assuming it accounted for everyone who may have had contact with the gems since they'd come into the auction house's possession.

And yes, he'd checked the guest list of all the parties where the Blueblood Burglar had struck, and while the only name on all seven guest lists had been Cass's, Marcos's name had appeared on six of them. And the party that Marcos had not attended was one thrown by a Melina Rebisi Parker.

After making a quick cell phone call to Bunnie Bernaldo while en route to the station, Sam found out Melina Parker was indeed Marcos's sister. Her brother could have stolen the Tiffany watch from her home at any point. The theft hadn't occurred during the Parkers' party. Cass wasn't to blame.

Cursing himself, Sam rushed up to the outer desk at the holding cells.

"Cass Richards," he said to the jailer. "I want her in an interrogation room, now."

"No can do, Detective."

"What do you mean?" Sam glowered.

"She's not here."

Darkly, Sam leaned across the desk. "What do you mean she's not here?"

"Some guy sprang her about…" He checked his watch. "Forty-five minutes ago."

Sam fisted his hand. "Who? What guy?"

"Hang on." He tapped on the computer keyboard, consulted the screen in front of him. "Um…his name was Marcos Rebisi."

"THANK YOU SO MUCH for bailing me out of jail, Marcos."

"You're welcome."

They were standing in the kitchen of Cass's apartment. Marcos had given her a ride home in his Porsche. He'd arrived to post her bail at the same moment the jailer had been escorting her to a phone to call Morgan. She'd been uncomfortable letting Marcos bail her out, considering she didn't want to encourage his thinking that they could get back together again. But she'd been even less comfortable staying in jail.

"By the way, how did you know I'd been arrested?"

she asked, the thought occurring to her for the first time. She had just been so thankful to leave that cement cell and those lonely black bars behind that she hadn't asked too many questions.

Marcos smiled. "I keep tabs on my favorite girl."

"Keep tabs?" Cass frowned. What did he mean by that?

He moved closer to her.

Unsettled, Cass stepped back.

"I've been keeping a close eye on you."

She gulped. "You've been spying on me? Stalking me?"

"No, no." Marcos shook his head. "I would never do anything to frighten you. I've just been watching over you, protecting you. Waiting for you to come to your senses and realize how much you love me."

He reached out a hand to stroke her cheek. Cass shrank back against the kitchen cabinets. A knob poked her hard in the spine. He cupped the back of her head in his palm.

"I forgive you," he whispered. "Everything is all right now."

"Forgive me? For what?"

Marcos's too handsome face clouded darkly. "For getting cold feet and running out on me. I know you're scared of commitment. That's why I had to make sure that you would need me. So I could prove that I would always be there for you. No matter what. There's no need to be afraid."

"You," she said as understanding dawned. "You're the Blueblood Burglar."

"Yes," he said. "But when the police hardly paid any attention, I knew I had to do something more dramatic. I had to force their hand."

"So you robbed the auction house. You stole the jewelry from the Zoey Zander collection and you mailed it to me. And then you broke in, ransacked my apartment and planted the Blueblood Burglar loot in my milk carton."

"I didn't break in," he denied. "I used the key you gave me."

"I never gave you a key." In equal turns she felt both mad and scared.

"You left it out in plain sight when I came over to pick you up for a date one night while you were in your room getting ready. It was an open invitation to have a copy made."

"You're unbelievable." Her heart thudded and her mind raced. The man was obviously deranged.

"It was for your own good, Cassandra. Can't you see that?" Marcos stroked the underside of her jaw with his thumb.

She stiffened. "How is getting framed for burglary good for me?"

"So I could be there for you when you were arrested. I just never figured you'd cheat on me with that cop." He scowled. "But I can forgive you for that, too. I understand. You're a sexy woman and you have physical needs. But I'm here to meet them now."

"No, no, you're not."

"Yes." He was smiling again. "Yes I am."

He trailed a finger down the hollow of her throat to the top of her cleavage and it was all she could do not to shudder.

"You got your comeuppance," he said. "The cop betrayed you. He slept with you and then he arrested you. But I never will betray you, Cass, never. You should have made love to me and none of this would have happened. I hope you've learned your lesson."

And then she saw the gun.

The butt of it protruded from the waistband of his tailor-made trousers. At that point, she realized exactly how much trouble she was in.

A knocked sounded at the door.

Marcos and Cass both froze.

"Cass! Are you in there? It's me, Sam."

Her heart leapt. Frantically, she glanced at the door, trying to measure her chance for escape.

"I need to talk to you, Cass," Sam called. "It's very important. If you're in there, please open the door."

Marcos wrapped a hand around her upper arm, dug his fingers into her skin. "Tell the cop to go away. Tell him you never want to see him again. Tell him or I'll kill him."

His eyes flashed wildly and he pulled the gun from his waistband. Cass had no doubt that he meant business.

"Go away, Sam, I don't want to talk to you," she said, raising her voice loud enough so he could hear her through the thickness of the door.

"Cass, are you all right?"

Marcos's fingers bit harder into her flesh. Cass winced. "Answer him," he hissed in her ear.

"Yes, no thanks to you. Now go away."

"Listen, we really have to talk."

Marcos pointed the gun at the door. "Make him go away, Cass. Or I'll shoot through the door."

"He's a cop, you can't shoot him. It'd be capital murder."

Marcos swung the gun around, pointed it at Cass's temple. "Fine, I'll kill you and then I'll kill myself. One way or the other, we'll be together forever."

"No, Marcos. No killing." She held her hands up in a defensive gesture. "Calm down. I'll make him go away."

Her mind scrambled for some kind of a coded message. Something to give Sam a clue as to what was really going on. Something Marcos would not recognize.

Without a better plan, Cass ended up babbling and praying Sam would understand. "Sam Mason, you've forced me out on a ledge, knocked me off balance and you betrayed me. I hate you. I never want to see you again. Get away from my door. Get out of my apartment building. Get out of my life."

Dear God, she prayed, please don't let Sam think I really hate him.

Total silence from the other side of the door.

Marcos was still brandishing the gun. Aiming it first at the door, his jaw tight, his eyes red-rimmed, breathing heavy. Then the next second, he would swing the weapon around and direct it at her.

"Okay, Cass," Sam's steady voice came at last. She couldn't read anything into the sound of it. "If that's what you want. I'm leaving. I'll leave you alone."

She caught her breath.

They heard the sound of Sam's footsteps retreating down the hallway.

Cass exhaled.

Marcos grabbed her by the hair.

"Ow, what are you doing?" She swatted at him until he pressed the gun into her side.

"Be still."

"Stop pulling my hair."

He shoved her in front of him. "Into your bedroom," he said. "I'm going to get what's due me."

YOU'VE FORCED ME OUT ON A LEDGE.

Cass's words echoed in Sam's head. They made no sense. They were out of context. He thought of the window ledge at Isaac Vincent's where he'd first met her. How she'd knocked him off balance and they'd fallen together into the airbag. What was she saying?

His gut torqued. Something was wrong. Something was very wrong.

He realized she was sending him a signal. Marcos Rebisi must be in the apartment with her, holding her against her will.

As a cop, he was bound by the law. Cass had told him to go away. He had no evidence to support his suspicion Marcos was holding her hostage. He had no proof Marcos had done anything illegal. None at all. And yet, Sam just knew that he was in Cass's apartment and she wasn't able to speak freely or let him in.

Something in her voice, something in the way his

heart churned told him that Cass was in serious peril. No matter what words she used to chase him away, she did not want him to go.

But if he stayed and tried to force the issue, tried to make her let him in, Marcos could hurt her. Sam wasn't willing to take that risk.

The fire escape. He could get into her bedroom window through the fire escape.

Which meant he'd have to go up on the roof. His head spun.

It's time to get over your fear of heights. Cass is depending on you.

He'd gone out on a ledge for her once before, when he hadn't even known her. He'd do whatever it took to save her. He would rock the boat, he would violate the law, he would, by God, overcome his fear of heights.

Whatever it took.

He scaled the stairs up one more floor and stepped out onto the roof. Purposefully, he stalked to the edge. Sam stood on the brink, forcing himself to look down.

Hurry, you don't have much time. You don't know what's going on in that apartment or what he's doing to Cass.

Galvanized, Sam started down the fire escape.

He paid no attention to the wad of panic in his stomach and he ignored the shaking of the thin metal beneath his feet. By sheer will of effort, he pushed himself down those stairs until he reached Cass's bedroom window.

Cautiously, he bent to peer in.

What he saw froze his heart.

Marcos Rebisi was sitting on the edge of Cass's bed with a gun pointed at her chest, making her do a striptease.

ONE MINUTE CASS WAS EDGING her bra strap down over her shoulders, praying for divine intervention so she wouldn't have to have sex with Marcos, and the next minute her bedroom window shattered.

She screamed and fell to the floor, covering her head with her arms.

"Drop the gun, Rebisi."

Sam? Tentatively, she lowered her hands and raised her head.

Sam stood in the middle of her bedroom, his gun drawn, glass glistening in his hair, a cut on his cheek bleeding. His eyes were narrowed at Marcos, who was on her bed with both hands raised in the air, his gun resting on her pillow.

Cass jumped up, grabbed her discarded clothes and clutched them to her nearly naked body.

Sam strode across the room, confiscated Marcos's gun and then handcuffed him. He used her phone to call for backup. He made Marcos lie down on the bathroom floor and locked him in. Then he turned to Cass, took her clothes from her and gently began to dress her.

Teeth chattering with fear and cold from the wind blowing in her fractured bedroom window, she told him everything that had happened. When she'd finished and she was fully clothed again. Sam cupped her chin in his palm and held her gaze.

"Forgive me, Cass, for not believing you." Sam threaded the fingers of his right hand through her left, then raised their joined hands to his lips and gently kissed each knuckle.

"I understand, Sam. You were a cop, doing your job. Just like with your ex-wife."

"Except she was guilty and I knew it and you were innocent and in my gut, I knew that too. I don't trust my instincts enough. I'm too worried about making a stink or breaking the rules."

"It's okay, no harm, no foul."

"Are you kidding? If I hadn't arrested you, then you wouldn't have ended up in Rebisi's clutches."

"Yes, I would have. He's pathologically obsessed with me. One way or the other, he would have come after me."

"I let you down."

"No, you did not. You saved me."

"You saved yourself with that out-on-a-ledge clue." She grinned. "I was hoping you'd pick up on that."

"You're amazing," he whispered.

"You're the amazing one. Climbing my fourth-floor fire escape when you're afraid of heights."

"You know," he said, "I think I've conquered that fear."

"Hey, I'm just glad you showed up when you did." She cast an uneasy glance at the locked bathroom door. "A few minutes longer and Marcos would have compromised my virtue."

He held her close and she shivered against him. He stroked her head. "It's okay," he murmured. "It's all over now."

"I don't think I can stay here tonight. Not with all that's happened."

"You don't have to," he said. "I'm taking you home with me."

16

IT WAS SIX O'CLOCK in the evening when they arrived at Sam's house in Queens. They'd been at the 39th Precinct for hours, giving their statement, wrapping the case up.

During interrogation, Marcos had confessed to stealing the jewels from the Zoey Zander collection, but he swore that someone had robbed him while he was in the process of removing them from the auction house and this unknown person had stolen the White Star from him but left the rest of the loot behind.

His story was flimsy, but Sam did tell Cass about the blood from an anonymous source found on the onyx brooch. The DNA specimen had been filed and the mystery of the missing White Star went unsolved.

Cass was happy Sam had invited her to his house, but once the front door had closed behind them and she was totally alone with him, she suddenly found that she felt awkward and shy. She rarely felt shy around men and she and Sam had already shared their bodies with each other. There was no reason for a sudden attack of nerves, but there it was.

She was nervous and scared to death. Of what, she didn't exactly know.

Still, she would rather be here with him than anywhere else on earth.

She liked his house. It was masculine but clean. Leather furniture, sports memorabilia on the walls, lots of electronic gadgets and sensible Berber carpeting that wouldn't show beer and pizza stains. The place was him. Reliable, comfortable, homey.

Sam stood there looking as awkward as she felt.

A long silence filled his cozy living room and then they both spoke at once.

"Well, this is weird," Cass said at the same time Sam said, "I've got a surprise for you."

"A surprise?" It was such the right thing to say. She adored surprises. As long as it was a good surprise. "It is a good surprise, isn't it?"

"A good surprise."

"What is it?" She squirmed, delighted.

"Hang on." He disappeared into another room and then returned with a Doc Martens shoe box.

Ugh. Had he bought her a pair of Doc Martens? Cass forced a smile. Okay, she'd pretend to like them even if she didn't. He had after all done something very nice for her.

Sam handed her the shoe box, his face earnest, hopeful. In that moment, Cass realized exactly how vulnerable he was, going out on a limb by giving her a gift, waiting anxiously for her approval. His openness touched her. By gosh, she would love these frickin' Doc Martens as she'd never loved another pair of shoes.

She lifted the lid, peeled back the tissue paper and her heart melted. "My Manolos!"

He grinned.

Holding the shoe box in one hand, she threw an arm around his shoulders and hugged him tightly. "How did you find them?"

"When we got back from the Catskills, I talked to Bunnie and asked her to send her driver after them. They were pretty messed up from the rain so I sent them out to have them refurbished. I just got them back yesterday."

Her throat felt scratchy and her heart was so full. "Oh, Sam, that was so sweet of you."

"I know how much the shoes meant to you."

"This is just…" She had to stop talking or she was going to cry.

He took the shoe box from her grasp and set it on his coffee table. Sam smiled, stretched out a hand and any lingering doubt or awkwardness between them evaporated.

No one had ever taken her breath the way that he did. He wasn't heartbreaker handsome, but to her, he was the most breathtaking man. He kissed her. Gently, sweetly, like it was their first time.

She stroked his cheek with a fingertip.

He whispered sweet nothings in her ear and took her hand again. He guided her into his bedroom, dropping kisses on her face along the way. His dear cheek was cut from the broken glass, but someone at the police station had slapped a bandage on it for him.

They sat together on the edge of his big king-size bed gazing deeply into each other's eyes. He kissed her again. At first with little licks and nips, his lips gentle and damp across her eyelids and her cheeks.

When did he unbutton her blouse? She wondered this as his hands and then his mouth skated over her breasts. Shutting her eyes, she felt the slick silk fabric of her bra drift over her shoulders and heard it hit the ground behind her with a soft sound.

Her skirt fell to her feet and he moved beside her, his erection hard against her thigh. Nothing felt awkward now. It was all smooth and even as if it were happening in some romantic movie.

He shrugged out of his clothes.

More kisses. Deep and sweet and thirsty.

Cass broke the kiss and nibbled a trail down his chin to his throat to his chest and beyond.

When her mouth touched his jutting penis, he sucked in his breath. She raised her head and met his gaze. His eyes filled with wonder and fascination and desire as he watched her stroke him. He looked open, vulnerable, unlike the tough pragmatic cop she'd first met. She'd misjudged him and his ability to express emotion.

The heat of desire in his eyes was so stark, so hungry, it took her breath. He wanted her.

She could see it in his eyes. Could taste it on his lips. Felt it in his fingertips. He wanted her in a way no other man had ever wanted her.

And she wanted him more than she had ever wanted another.

While she was fondling him with her mouth, he lightly reached for her, his fingers skimming over her pelvic bone. She closed her eyes as she felt energy surge up from her feminine core into her breasts and into her throat. She tasted her own passion hot and ripe, mingling with the earthy flavor of him.

A silky moan escaped his lips. He carefully twisted away from her, breaking her gentle suction on his erection.

Her eyes flew open and she saw he had shifted onto his side, propping himself on his elbow. He was peering at her and she saw the raw, animal intensity of need in eyes the color of smoke.

He kissed her, his mouth urgent. His electricity filled her, shocked her. He was more powerful than a charge of white-hot lightning.

When he lightly grazed her most tender spot, a desperate sweetness suffused her body, full of opulent enchantment. And all the capacity of her desire sprang alive. She reached for him, seizing, eating greedily.

She had no more restraint. Abandon claimed her and she thrust herself against his hard body.

But he was gentle and caring. He acted as if she was going to snap into a million pieces if he so much as breathed on her.

She must have shut her eyes again because all she registered, remembered registering were sensations. Moist, soft, sweet, hot, hard, seep, slide, ooze, slick, hard, hard, hard, hot, hot, hot.

Cass enfolded her legs around his lean waist and

with a deferential groan, he plummeted into her. She felt so amazingly secure with him. She let go of control and let him carry her along with his masculine tempo. She surrendered, abundantly, wholly, without faltering. Unleashed her hesitation and relinquished everything to him.

She felt his penis and then his tongue and then his penis inside her again and again and again. He was everywhere but she was conscious only of the delicate tip of steel that this ardent man, darkly radiant with desire for her, was drawing down the center of her being.

The orgasm was large inside her. So massive. Spreading and spiraling. A wildfire. Out of control. The air vibrated a chorus. Humming his praises. "Sam, Sam, Sam."

The sensation rushed through her melodious, deepness, hot, intense, flaming, burning like a slant of dazzling light far up inside her, diffusing through her and fanning in starbursts of joy.

She shattered against him as he shattered into her.

"Oh, Sam." She breathed. "Sam."

"I love you, Cass," he whispered. "With all my heart and soul. I love you."

CASS FLOPPED OVER onto her back, listening to the sound of her blood rushing through her ears. Sam was breathing nice and steady and she timed her breaths to match.

Holding her hand directly above his hip bone, she absorbed the sensation of his body heat radiating up through her palm. She cataloged everything about him—the texture of his skin, so smooth and thick and tanned, the color of his hair, a tasty shade of oatmeal cookie dough, the fragrance of his pores, a meaty, masculine smell that made her want to lick him. She noticed how the very quality of the air in the room seemed different because they were breathing in tandem.

She'd learned so much about him in such a short amount of time. He's gifted me with grace, she thought.

Her eyes misted and an odd airiness inflated her heart. She was overcome with sadness so overwhelming she feared she could die from the loneliness of it.

Her natural instinct was to joke, to dance, to giggle. Anything to elevate her frame of mind and jam the gloominess. But this time, Cass sought none of her usual defenses against melancholia. Instead she experienced the emotions, knotted her hands into fists and let it come. The sorrow rolled over her, through her, past her and she came out on the other side reborn.

She was not destroyed by experiencing the uncomfortable sensations as she always feared she'd be if she wallowed too much in her feelings. Rather she was liberated, recognizing that emotions were nothing more than transient states of being she could chose to face and accept or run away from and deny.

She'd been running for too long.

All these years what she thought passed for happiness—high fashion and hanging with the "in" crowd and dating men who looked good standing next to her—was alien to this sudden imperturbable sense of conviction. Her understanding of honest happiness had been forever altered.

She had changed.

And she realized something startling. Without commitment she would never learn to care for another person more than she cared for herself.

In that iridescent moment resplendent in the glow of their lovemaking, Cass knew what she must do. She had to quit running from pain. She had to embrace it and then renounce it. What she had been fleeing had occurred and she'd survived.

Last night, Sam had told her that he loved her. She hadn't said it back to him, because words weren't going to be enough. Not for him and not for her. She needed a concrete symbol, something that would prove, beyond a shadow of a doubt that she was changed.

But what?

And how?

Was she truly ready for this step?

She'd spent a lifetime living for herself and now there was someone else to consider, someone whose happiness meant more to her than her own.

In order to move ahead, she had to make a sacrifice. She had to let go of her past, of her fears. She'd been an inmate of her own emotional prison for far too long. It was time to let go.

And thanks to Sam, she finally understood how.

WHEN THE DAWN SUNLIGHT slanting through his bedroom window awakened Sam, he rolled over, reaching for Cass, only to find her gone. He sprang upright in bed, not knowing what to think, cocking his head, listening for sounds of her.

"Cass?"

No answer.

He threw off the covers, slipped on his underwear and padded through the house, knowing he would not find her hiding in the closet or giggling behind the curtains, but he looked anyway. Hoping against hope she was playing a game and hadn't run away from him.

Dammit. He'd screwed everything up.

Why had he told her he loved her? He'd known she wasn't ready to hear those monumental words and yet he'd stupidly let the words fall from his lips in the throes of happy lovemaking.

He sank down on his couch, not knowing what to do and that's when he noticed the shoe box he'd given her the night before was missing. No doubt about it. She'd taken her shoes and walked out.

Should he leave her be? Obviously, she hadn't been able to handle his declaration of love.

Part of him whispered, "Don't rock the boat." It was a piece of his personality that had dominated too much of his life. He thought of the times he'd checked out and put his own life on hold. The times when he hadn't rocked the boat that needed a good rocking, how he'd missed out on a lot of good things because he hadn't wanted to risk the discomfort of instability. He'd been on an even keel far too long.

He wasn't going to leave this alone. He was going

to find Cass and tell her exactly how he felt. And if she rejected him, well he would deal with it. But at least he would have taken a stand, expressed his wants and desires for once instead of putting someone else's needs above his own simply for the sake of keeping the peace.

Sam took a deep breath. He was not only ready to go out on a limb for Cass, but to saw it off if that's what it took.

Galvanized into action, he reached for the telephone. He called Cass's house but had no luck. Not satisfied with leaving a message on her machine, he then called the precinct and asked the desk clerk to look up Cass's file and give him her sister's phone number. Five minutes later, he was on the phone with Morgan Shaw.

"Have you heard from Cass?" he asked after he'd introduced himself.

"Yes," Morgan said. "And I'm worried about her. She didn't sound like her usual self."

"What do you mean?"

"She sounded…well, this may seem strange to you, but she sounded grounded."

"Is that a bad thing?"

"I don't know."

They lapsed into a short silence, both considering the implications of a grounded Cass.

"Do you know where she might be?" Sam asked. "I called her apartment but she's not answering the phone."

"She said there were things she had to do. She said she was going to call in to work and take the rest of the week off."

"Did she tell you where she was going?"

"No."

"Thanks for your help," he said.

"Sam?"

"Yeah."

"I think Cass sounding grounded is a very good thing and I think it's all due to you."

"You give me too much credit," he said but her words warmed his heart.

"No," Morgan said. "I don't think you're giving yourself enough credit. She's changed a lot since she met you."

"Really?"

"Do you love her, Sam?"

"You have no idea how much."

"Then find her, Sam, tell her how much you love her and no matter what she does to push you away, don't let her go."

Thanking Morgan for her advice, Sam hung up.

He took the subway to Cass's apartment, praying she was there, his mind flashing between the wonderful memories of last night and his conversation with Morgan. His gut churned with equal amounts of excitement and fear. What was Cass doing? Where was she going? And why had she taken time off from work?

Holding his breath, he pushed through the door into her building.

And saw a cleaning lady organizing her supplies, Cass's Hermès scarf wrapped gaily around her neck.

"Excuse me," he said, approaching the woman. "Where did you get that scarf?"

She stopped what she was doing, looked up at him and fingered the scarf with a happy smile on her face. "A lady who lives in the building gave it to me to wear to a job interview. I think it'll bring me good luck. I sure need some."

"I'm sure it will," Sam said.

"Cass Richards—that's her name—she's the kindest person."

"That she is. Do you know if she's home?" He pointed at the staircase.

The woman shook her head, grinning. "She just left the building."

"Thanks," Sam said and then got the hell out of there before tears came to his eyes.

To think that Cass, a woman who not two weeks earlier had risked her very life to hold on to that expensive designer scarf, had just freely and generously given it away to a woman who needed it more than she. In that moment, he loved Cass more than he ever thought possible.

"HERE'S THE DEAL, NIKKI." Cass knelt at her old friend's grave, their high school photograph and the Doc Marten shoe box with her Manolos inside clutched to her chest. "I'm going to ask you to forgive me for being a wimp. I'm sorry I couldn't handle our friendship when you needed it most."

She reached out and trailed her fingertips over Nikki's

headstone, tracing the etched dates. "But I'm stronger now. I've become a better person and if I could do it all over again, I'd stick by you every step of the way."

Rocking back on her heels, Cass placed the picture in the shoe box and put the shoe box on Nikki's grave. She took a shaky breath and brushed tears from the corners of her eyes before she could continue. It would be so easy to stop talking, to take back her shoes and return to her life the way it had been before Sam. But she could not. Cass was done with taking the easy way out.

"I found out—" she swallowed "—that if I want to experience real happiness then I have to give up pursuing it and just be happy. And if I want love, then I'm going to have to open up and let myself feel love."

In that present moment, at Nikki's grave, Cass at long last gave herself permission to grieve. All these years she'd been avoiding expressing her sorrow over what she had lost. But in her avoidance of pain, she had also avoided true and lasting joy.

With tears streaming down her cheeks, she stood up, dusted off her knees, then slowly turned and walked away. Leaving behind her Manolo Blahniks, leaving the photograph, letting go of the guilt and forgiving herself for being flawed.

"I CAN'T FIND HER, Beth, and I'm going insane." Sam paced Beth's sunny yellow kitchen. "I'm worried. Marcos Rebisi said someone knocked him on the head and took the White Star. What if whoever took the amulet is after Cass?"

"Calm down, big brother. Why would the White Star thief be after Cass?"

"I don't know. I'm just…frustrated." He shoved a hand through his hair. "And worried about her."

"And in love," Beth finished.

"Yeah." Sam flung himself down in a chair. "I'm stone cold in love with her."

Beth patted his hand. "It's going to work out."

"I don't see how. She ran away from me and I don't know why. She's not answering her cell phone. I've been by her apartment three times already. I should never have told her I loved her. I knew she had trouble with commitment. I was moving too fast. Damn, damn, damn." He pounded his palm against his forehead.

Beth chuckled.

He raised his head and glared at her. "What's so damned funny?"

"Seeing you so twisted up." She shook her head.

"My suffering amuses you?"

"No, no." She got up and came over to massage his tense shoulders. "I love seeing you so passionate about someone. You always tried so hard not to care too much. Probably because of what happened to Janie. You never wanted to feel that kind of hurt again. Look how disconnected you were from Keeley. It took you months to figure out what she was up to. But this woman, she's lit a spark in you that I haven't seen since before Janie's accident. She's truly something special."

"Okay, but how do I hold on to her without chasing her away?"

"From what you've told me about Cass, I don't think it's commitment that really scares her. I think it's a fear of being out of control. What you need is a grand gesture to prove to her that you don't want to change her or turn her into something she's not. You've got to let her know you accept her exactly as she is, and if that means you have to let go of the idea of an official commitment like an engagement or marriage, then you have to let it go."

Beth had hit upon the truth. The minute she said it, Sam knew. "How'd you get so smart, baby sister?"

"I had a wonderful big brother who taught me a lot."

Sam got up, hugged Beth. "Thanks for your advice."

"Where are you going?" she asked as he headed for the door.

He grinned. "I've got a grand gesture to plan."

CASS WENT BACK TO WORK with her head clear and her heart lighter than it had ever been. She'd tried to call Sam upon her return, but he hadn't answered his phone. She'd told herself it was okay. That even if nothing more happened between them, he'd given her what she needed most and she would never ever forget him for that. Part of her couldn't help hoping for a happy ending, but she wouldn't push, she wouldn't pursue happiness at full throttle, she'd just experience life and let things happen the way they were supposed to happen.

"Cass, Cass." Mystique came running into her office.

Cass looked up from the PR campaign she was working on, revolving around star-crossed lovers inspired by the French book she'd found in Morgan's antique shop, and she felt it was the most creative work she'd ever done.

"What is it, Mystique?"

Mystique pushed her way to the window. "Come look down."

Cass frowned. "I'm sort of busy right now."

"It can wait. Come look down."

"All right." Cass sighed and pushed back from her desk.

Giggling, Mystique opened the window. Traffic noises blew in. "Come look down."

Grumbling, Cass crossed the room to join Mystique at the window. "What's so important that you've got to interrupt me right in the middle of—" She broke off at what she saw directly below the eight-floor window.

Oh. My. God.

There in the middle of Broadway traffic was parked a shiny red fire truck with a very long ladder propped against the side of the brownstone. And three quarters of the way up the ladder climbed a man with a cake in his hand.

But not just any man and not just any cake.

It was Sam.

Her brave, handsome, scared-of-heights-but-not-going-to-let-it-stop-me Sam.

Balancing in one arm a three-tiered chocolate Barbie cake with M&M's and sprinkles.

Cass began trembling all over. Two more rungs and his face appeared in her window. He placed the cake on the window ledge and grinned at her.

"Sam Mason," she cried. "What the hell are you doing?"

"Grand gesture," he said.

"But you're afraid of heights."

"Not half as afraid as I am of losing you. But don't worry. I'm not here to ask you for a commitment," he said.

"You're not?"

"Nope. We haven't known each other long enough for you to feel secure about my feelings for you."

"We haven't?"

"When you're ready for more, you'll let me know."

"What if it takes me a long time?"

"I'm a patient guy. I'll wait."

"What if something's broken inside me, Sam? What if I can't ever commit?"

"You're not broken, Cass, you're just scared. You think you can't commit, when the truth is you were already committed."

"What are you talking about?"

"You were already committed to your footloose way of life. The way I see it you're a shoe-in to do fifty or sixty years of marriage, just as soon as you realize it."

"Get in here," she said, picking up the cake and handing it to Mystique. "Before you hurt your silly self."

She held out her hand and he took it as he climbed through the window and into her office. Applause sounded behind them and they looked around to find the employees of Isaac Vincent standing in her doorway.

But she didn't care. She only had eyes for Sam. A man who loved her enough to face his greatest fear. A man who wanted her badly enough to accept her exactly as she was, with no strings or commitments.

Her heart was giddy.

Sam. Sam's the man.

She threw her arms around his neck and kissed him. "Actually, I came to the same conclusion you did."

Cass looked into Sam's eyes and saw her best self the way he saw her.

When she was with him she felt transcended. She had it now. She understood. She'd learned to stop glossing over the surface of life, to assimilate her experiences in depth. She'd learned to appreciate, be grateful and enthralled by the wonders all around her. Through Sam she'd developed a sense of the boundless goodness of life. She'd taken that leap of faith and learned true love had been waiting to catch her when she faltered.

She told him all this and so much more.

"So what are you saying Cass?"

"I'm saying I'm ready for whatever the future brings. With you, there's nothing to be afraid of."

Sam kissed her again and Cass grabbed hold of her happily-ever-after with both hands.

"I love you, Sam," she whispered. "I love you, I love you, I love you."

And in dedicating herself to one path, one cake, one man, her life was made whole.

IN A LAVISH VILLA in the south of France, high on a hill overlooking the Mediterranean Sea, an obsession grew.

A dark dangerous obsession that promised to ruin all who came in contact with it.

He must have the White Star at all costs. She was the only thing that could save him. Without her, he was cursed forever.

And with her, his life would be transformed.

Where was that miserable Jean Allard? He cursed the day he'd hired that worthless thief. Two weeks he'd been waiting. Two weeks since Allard had called and told him he'd successfully taken the White Star from the Zoey Zander collection at the Stanhope auction house.

But then not another word.

He paced his elaborate study decorated in marble and leather and cherry wood and rare books. He had everything in the world except what he wanted most.

He paced and he drank expensive whiskey and he cursed and lived his dark secret. The secret no one could ever know. The secret only the White Star could cure.

He had to have the amulet.

Time was running out.

Something had to be done. He would get her, no matter what the cost, and if anyone got in his way, he would kill them.

* * * * *

Look for HIDDEN GEMS by Carrie Alexander,
coming next month from Harlequin Blaze,
when Marissa's story unfolds and the hunt for the
White Star heats up....

A Special Treat from Blaze...

Sex or chocolate. Which is better?

This Valentine's Day, join three of Blaze's bestselling authors in proving that in both sex and chocolate, too much of a good thing...is a good thing!

SINFULLY SWEET

contains

Wickedly Delicious by Janelle Denison
Constant Craving by Jacquie D'Alessandro
Simply Scrumptious by Kate Hoffmann

A Decadent Valentine's Day Collection

On sale February 2006

If you enjoyed what you just read,
then we've got an offer you can't resist!

Take 2 bestselling
love stories FREE!
Plus get a FREE surprise gift!

HARLEQUIN®

COMING NEXT MONTH

#231 GOING ALL OUT Jeanie London
Red Letter Nights

Bree Addison never dreamed that landing in Lucas Russell's yard would change everything. Who knew that her rescuer would be bent on having a sizzling affair with her? And who could have guessed that her nights would suddenly become one big sensual adventure? Only, adventures aren't meant to last....

#232 ROOM SERVICE Jill Shalvis
Do Not Disturb

It should be simple. All TV producer Em Harris has to do is convince chef Jacob Hill to sign on for her new culinary show. Only, when she sets foot in Hush, the sex-themed hotel where Jacob works, she knows she's in over her head. Especially when she develops an irresistible craving for the sinfully delicious chef...

#233 TALL, TANNED & TEXAN Kimberly Raye
24 Hours: Island Fling

After years of trying to make cowboy Rance McGraw notice her, Deanie Codge is taking action! Two weeks at Camp E.D.E.N., a notorious island retreat, will teach her to unleash her inner sex kitten. The next time she sees her cowboy, she'll be ready. And it turns out to be sooner than she thinks....

#234 SINFULLY SWEET Janelle Dension, Jacquie D'Alessandro, Kate Hoffmann
A Decadent Valentine's Day Collection

Sex or chocolate. Which is better? This Valentine's Day, join three of Blaze's bestselling authors in proving that, in both sex *and* chocolate, too much of a good thing…is a good thing!

#235 FLIRTATION Samantha Hunter
The HotWires, Bk. 3

EJ Beaumont is one big flirt. Not exactly the best trait for a cop, but it's an asset on his current computer crime investigation. He's flirting big-time with a sexy online psychic who—rumor has it—is running a lonely-hearts scam. Only problem is, as a psychic, Charlotte Gerard has EJ's number but good!

#236 HIDDEN GEMS Carrie Alexander
The White Star, Bk. 2

Jamie Wilson thinks his best friend, Marissa Suarez, is dating the wrong men—his wanting her for himself has *nothing* to do with his opinion. When Marissa's apartment suddenly becomes a target for thieves, Jamie steps up to the plate. Maybe Marissa will finally see the hidden gem he is—inside the bedroom and out!

www.eHarlequin.com

HBCNM0106